Now...a
Harlequin
romance
by Anne Mather
comes to life
on the movie screen

starring
KEIR DULLEA · SUSAN PENHALIGON

Leopard in the Snow

Guest Stars
KENNETH MORE · BILLIE WHITELAW

featuring GORDON THOMSON as MICHAEL
and JEREMY KEMP as BOLT

Produced by JOHN QUESTED and CHRIS HARROP
Screenplay by ANNE MATHER and JILL HYEM
Directed by GERRY O'HARA

An Anglo-Canadian Co-Production

OTHER
Harlequin Romances
by JOYCE DINGWELL

Year of the Dragon

by

JOYCE DINGWELL

Harlequin Books

TORONTO • LONDON • NEW YORK • AMSTERDAM • SYDNEY

Original hardcover edition published in 1977
by Mills & Boon Limited

ISBN 0-373-02164-X

Harlequin edition published May 1978

Printed in U.S.A.

CHAPTER ONE

THROUGH the window of the college residence hall Clo could see the Star Ferry bearing down on the wharf at Victoria, and she knew that if she were to collect the new lecturer from Kowloon's Hotel Stella she had better leave at once.

It was only a short stroll, and the Star would take twice that time to berth and disgorge, but Clo was aware that even after a lifetime here, *her* lifetime, she remained capable of missing a boat, an appointment, anything, simply by looking at and listening to and being in Hong Kong.

Hong Kong. Hong Kong was a silk cheongsam, Clo always thought; it was stimulation, excitement, fluidity, vitality, the clop of wooden pattens, the lilt of Cantonese, spicy cooking, secret smiles, pure fascination. She had never stopped being fascinated. She knew she never would.

She descended the stairs, stepped out of the privately endowed college block, and started determinedly down the hill, determined not to linger at the little shops selling embroidered fabrics, jade and porcelain, *not* to dawdle under the temple flower hedges where the children gathered the cream frangipanni petals to brew a magic tea, *not* to stop to admire the effect of young gold cheeks suffused with wild rose, but to catch the Star instead.

Clo did ... but just. The Star had to be held up for her, and the boat boy, close-shorn in his summer hair style, for there were two styles per year, normal for winter, crew short for summer, gave her a gamin look. If she had been older and more elegant, Clo knew he would have whispered remindingly: *'Tippu?'* But she was not, so he smiled, and

Clo smiled back, and the Star began to churn up snowy froth.

It was a mile-wide crossing to Kowloon, which meant Nine Dragons, referring to the nine granite foothills that once had circled it but now had whittled away. Clo always thought of it, though fondly, as Kowloon the raffish, as compared to Hong Kong, which meant Fragrant Harbour. She enjoyed Kowloon, it had more breath, more heartbeat than Victoria, but Fragrant Harbour came first with her. She looked back on the shining waters that now had a six-way traffic tunnel beneath them, and wondered how the Australian lecturer she was to pick up would think of it all. As a silk cheongsam? As clop and lilt and fascination? Come to consider it, how *did* Australians think? An Australian herself, she had not a clue. She had been three weeks old when her father had taken up this Hong Kong appointment and brought his wife and baby daughter to the Orient. Her mother had died when Clo was quite young, but the small family had not returned to Australia. The sweetest memories were here, Doctor Denning had always claimed, so why leave them? Besides, there was never a dearth of devoted amahs for the child. He loved it, and Clo had loved it. She was Australian, she supposed, but for three weeks only, and that was now twenty years ago.

As a matter of special interest to Clo, this was the first time she had been asked to collect an Australian—indeed, apart from Father, she hadn't even met one. She expected Australians would be represented at the University, but her own college contacts without variation had been either American or English. What did she know about Australia? Bondi Beach? The Opera House? She giggled, and the boat boy gave an even wider smile.

... 'Good afternoon, Professor,' Clo rehearsed inside her, 'welcome to Hong Kong. I'm here to take you across to your apartment in Victoria, "Victoria Hong Kong side", the tourists say. The tunnel is now complete, but you will soon agree that the Star Ferry is the charming way. How is Bondi? How is the Opera House?'

The Star Ferry belched and began to churn again, and Clo saw that Kowloon the raffish was looming up.

As well as being raffish, Kowloon was more exciting than Victoria. It might be seedy, but life spun at a more thrilling pace. It was literally crammed with shabby streets selling the whole world, or so it seemed, and if even then you could not find what your heart desired, you asked the rickshaw boy. The rickshaw boys, dried-up, stringy old men by day, rather fascinatingly roguish young men by night, could always tell you. 'Lickshaw? Good tea shop with cake? I show?' ... That was daytime. 'Lickshaw? Nice bar? Velly nice girl? I show?' ... That was night.

Clo always patronised the rickshaw boys. She was confident that her knowing manner and unspectacular ... to the rickshaw boys' eyes ... dress would stop her from being charged twice what she should be. Also, she knew that these human beasts of burden in their straw hats, blue shorts and jackets needed her fare. Also ... well, she liked the mode of travel. Rickshaw-riding was wonderful. It was comfortable in the hooded interior with its fresh white seat covers, and the rolling easy pace was sheer delight. Besides, rickshaw boys knew everything ... including much further than the rightful distance from the ferry to the Hotel Stella. Clo scolded her boy about that.

She got out and turned into one of the largest and best-known caravanserais, and that included the high-rise glitter palaces that were going up every day. But the college, who were sticklers, still patronised the Stella, and Clo could not remember how many men of learning she had greeted here, then escorted across to Victoria Hong Kong side. But this time it was different. This man of learning was her first Australian, and ... yes, it had to be admitted ... she disliked him in advance. She was ashamed of it, but she did. It was an unannounced but public fact that he was here eventually to oust her ~~ad.

'There's nothing official yet, Clo,' Doctor Denning had said one evening, 'but this young Ferrier will be coming to learn the ropes.'

'*Your* ropes.'

'Clo, I'm well in my sixties. You were an autumn child.'

'But your brain is as fine as ever,' she insisted.

'And my body going steadily down—yes, Clo, that is so. I've intended to talk to you on this subject many times. Clo, I can't last for ever.'

'You can last another twenty years.'

'... Or twenty months? Twenty days?'

'What are you saying, Dad?'

'I'm joking, of course. Now this young Professor Harry Ferrier ... I like the name of Harry ... free, like the wind.'

'How young?'

'A nice age for you.'

'Dad, in all the years I've known you I've never heard you matchmake!' scolded Clo. 'Only the Cantonese do that.'

'Have to do something when the writing's on the wall. Joking again, Clo.'

'Yes,' Clo had said, but in a slightly caught-up voice.

In the end it had all come down to this, as it always came down to this: a slight, acorn-haired girl in a denim skirt, white blouse and sandals walking into the glitter of the Stella, passing by the pillars, the caryatids, the potted palms and the busy bellhops in pillbox caps to ask at Reception: 'Professor Ferrier, please.'

... Thank heaven, Clo thought, as she waited on the thick carpet under the glittering chandeliers, that Reception knew her. Pretty Ah Ming ... Ming was the family name and prefixed by Ah ... had helped her before, and she smiled now and inquired: 'Shall I page?' to which Clo replied:

'No, if he's around, just show me.' Scholars, she had established, were a shy breed, and disliked being called over an address system.

'Yes. Over there. By the waterfront window. He's speaking to——' But Clo had gone. She had seen a dark head above a potted palm looking out of the window. In the spreading fronds of the palm she did not see anyone else, and anyhow, by the time she reached the man's side, he was standing alone.

So this was what Australians looked like, thought Clo the Australian.

Tall ... she had expected that. More slim than burly ... she had not expected that.

Then the skin, not bronzed as she had anticipated, more an exceedingly deep cream. And smooth. Somehow she had not thought of any Australian as smooth, more—well, rough.

Still, people were not peas in a pod, and especially, in spite of what visitors said, these Cantonese people. They had different eyes, different expressions, different——

The man was turning. Why, he was almost—well, un-English. She did not know much about un-Australian yet. Still, no one on earth, she reminded herself fairly, was a pea in a pod. She stepped forward.

'I'm sorry if you've been waiting,' she said. 'If we leave at once I think we can catch the next Star.'

'Star?'

He had a very correct voice, even for a lecturer, she had rather anticipated a slow, somewhat amused drawl. Still, she saw, if obliquely, he *was* amused, though definitely in a superior, patronising way. The glint of it showed in his extremely dark eyes, and it did *not* amuse Clo. Also she had supposed the eyes would be Anglo-Saxon blue or grey, but they were near-black.

'We could take a lickshaw' ... oh, help, what had got into her? ... 'I mean a rickshaw, but it's not far, the traffic is heavy, so we'd do better to walk.' She did not tell him her real reason, that reason being that though a rickshaw could hold two it did it very tightly, if not exactly cheek to cheek, then certainly body to body; also that she was conscious of her denim against his expensive heavy cream silk.

'Hurry,' she said, forgetting she had not introduced herself, forgetting she had not asked his name. 'This way, please.'

'To a star?' Again the crisp correct voice surprised her.

'The Star Ferry,' she explained. 'There's a tunnel, too. Under the harbour. But we're going above not below. Come along.'

To Clo's relief, Professor Harry Ferrier did.

The shabby streets that at nights became rivers of light were now just shabby streets. Kowloon put on all its raucous clamour, grime and stuffy smells for the tall man beside her. Jealous for her Orient, Clo hoped he noticed as well as the disadvantages the feathered eyebrows and blue-black hair of the lovely young girls passing by, their eyes demurely down except for one fleeting glance, the dear old men with their fans and umbrellas, the neat Cantonese women in tunic and trousers and wearing a gilt pin in their dark coiffures, the children ... ah, the children! For surely there were no children like these. Delicious doll girls with topknots, bullet-headed little boys in blue trousers, dimples at the corners between all their fingers, burnt-gold dimples to match their tiny burnt-gold hands.

'We'll just make the ferry.' For some inexplicable reason, Clo began to run. She could not have said why she felt unrelaxed in the new professor's presence, always she was an easy talker, and one would have thought that two Australians, even if one of them could not remember the country, would have much in common. The professor did not run with her, he just stretched his legs, and she knew she must look ridiculous scurrying a yard ahead.

That yard, alas, did it. If she had not run, if they had kept strictly equal, the boy on the pavement would have respected her and not intoned in his sing-song Cantonese lilt to the man behind her: 'Plenty nice girl. Shanghai girl. Portuguese girl. I show?'

The man stiffened. Clo had the distinct feeling he stiffened at the Portuguese part, so perhaps he had a Portuguese acquaintance . . .

'Quickly!' she said, and signalled the Star Ferry, about to pull out again. The same boat boy was in attendance, and he gave Clo a different look this time, a definite '*tippu*' look. After all, there was a gentleman with missie. Clo heard rather than saw her companion pass over some money.

· She began to talk frantically, telling him all about Kowloon, Victoria, the New Territories. In between her chatter she cast him apprehensive glances. No, not at all what she had expected, more proud, more straight, more dark, much more aloof. Arrogant features. Black eyes but with a fire somewhere in them. Darkly cream skin. A—foreign look.

He did not appear to notice her covert stares, and he did not speak until, having run through everything else, Clo started on Macao, forty miles west, on the Pearl River, established as a Portuguese settlement over four hundred years ago.

'Yes? Macao?' he asked.

'It's Portuguese,' Clo repeated rather wretchedly, 'area five square miles, not a—well, nice place.' She had not meant to say that, but his long silence had frazzled her.

'Nice?' he queried.

'Shady reputation . . . you know.'

'No, I don't know.'

'Not only gambling—another sort of thing.'

'What sort of thing?'

'Fan-tan,' Clo said desperately, 'games of chance.'

'*What sort of thing?*'

'We're here.' Clo got up, and he rose as well.

They climbed the hill to the hall of residence, as the college accommodation was known, and Clo told the Professor that he might be asked to guest-speak at the Chinese University in the New Territories upon occasion; as her father did.

'Our flats ... yours will be a bachelor one ... are quite plain, like most educational accommodation. Swedish influence, you know.'

Yes, he knew.

'We add our own bits and pieces. I have some lovely vases. Because you looked bare—I mean your flat did—I got Ah Seng to bring you one.'

'One?' he queried.

'A vase.'

'I see. And Ah Seng?'

'Your amah.'

He said coldly: 'I'm not a child.'

'No, but there's not too much work around for amahs now, zero population and all that, so amahs are doing other things as well. Don't worry' ... with an attempt at frivolity ... 'she won't serve you coddled eggs, in fact the only amah part about her will be her uniform with its piping round the edge of the tunic to show she's a baby nurse. She wouldn't part with that.'

'Why do I have her?' asked Professor Ferrier.

'You have to have her, you have to have someone, everyone does,' Clo explained.

'And if I don't want to?'

'You have her. Her husband had a junk and in it was a

tallow candle. One night the light caught the flimsy wood-work and everything went.' Clo paused. 'Including the father.'

'Any children?' he asked.

'Five. One child went to the victim's brother, one child went to his sister, one to his widow, Ah Seng's, brother, one to Ah Seng's sister——'

'Making four?' he prompted.

'The fifth remained with Ah Seng. He is Second Son. There are three boys and two girls in the family, and you will have Second Son. A very nice age, seven, don't you think?'

'*I* will have him?'

'He'll sleep in your little boxroom, you won't know he's there. He won't eat much.'

'How do you know all this?'

'Because we, my father and I, had him before you. We hate to let him go, but——'

'But?'

'But poor Ah Seng's brother died,' Clo told him, 'so his widow and her children and Ah Seng's own child who was being looked after by her brother's wife had nowhere to go.'

'So you took them?'

'Yes.'

'And then passed Ah Seng and Second Son on to me?'

'We have a larger flat, so we could accommodate the bigger number,' she explained.

'You mean without consulting me you've provided me with a housekeeper and a child?' he demanded.

'You had to have someone, everyone does. If you don't, you lose face.' Clo wondered a little hysterically if a haughty man like this could ever lose face. 'Orientals think a lot of face,' she said hurriedly. 'Here we are now.'

She led the way in, remembering too late that she had

not asked her rehearsed questions: Is it true koalas don't drink water? that emus have on occasion reached forty miles an hour?

She saw him glancing to right and left as he climbed to the second floor, a supercilious glance, she judged, for undoubtedly this superior Australian gentleman had come a long, long way from early colonial wattle and daub.

All the same it made her nervous, and she babbled again: 'Swedish. Basic. Very hygienic. I've told Amah to bring the blue vase.'

Clo barely finished her reassurance. They had reached the door of the bachelor flat, opened it and gone in. Ah Seng stood waiting for them; unlike the shy girls in the street with their demure downcast looks her weather-wrinkled face was wreathed in a welcoming smile.

To Clo's surprise … and a little mollification … the man smiled back, stepped forward and graciously extended his hand … only it never reached the amah; there must have been something dropped on the floor, either that or Ah Seng had polished too much, for instead he fell.

Ah Seng let out a scream, but it was not for her new master, it was for the vase that had become dislodged from the table in the commotion, and now lay in pieces on the floor.

'Bloken,' she wept.

'The Master,' protested Clo, badly frightened by the man's prone position, 'our new professor, Professor Harry Ferrier—fetch a doctor, Ah Seng, fetch a doctor quick-quick!'

'Your father Master Denning doctor,' pointed out Ah Seng.

'Fetch a *bone* doctor, Ah Seng. Quick!'

'But new master all well,' dismissed the amah, 'only vase bloken. Finish. No good. But new master well.'

'Ah Seng, the *doctor*!'

Ah Seng went out, carrying the pieces and weeping, and Clo turned her attention to the man on the floor.

She gave him an initial brief examination. Nothing seemed wrong, but he had a superficial cut on his forehead and he probably would suffer a headache. What about—other parts?

She gingerly slid off his safari type jacket, wondering again at that deeply cream skin, almost the same colour as the deep cream silk. No, everything seemed all right.

Now she did not just go gingerly, she practically trod on eggs. This might be the relaxed end of the century, and she might have been reared as a modern girl, but Clo still did not know about Australians and how they might react to—well, putting it bluntly, to having their trousers removed. Still, it had to be done. The doctor might be some time in coming for the simple reason that Ah Seng might take her time in telling, and if anything could be done to help him before medical aid arrived, she must do it.

Clo tried to undo a zip, to force a seam, but when he stirred and groaned from the effort she simply decided that this was it, and found some scissors and cut him out instead. Ah Seng's gasp beside her told Clo that the amah had returned—though not with the doctor but another vase. Her protest also was not about morals but waste.

'Velly good pants,' she said aghast, 'all cut up, all finish.'

'I had to. He's injured. He's sick, Ah Seng.'

'He's all well, master's all well, little knock but no finish. Vase finish. All bloken.'

'Ah Seng——' began Clo ... then she stopped. Stopped abruptly. For the first time really she was looking at the man, looking at what the scissors had done. They had cut up a very elegant, very expensive suit, but Clo was not staring at that. She was not staring either at the quality of the beautiful underwear, instead she was staring at a crest on the underwear. Like all crests, it was not at all obvious.

Clo could only establish a tree ... a cork tree, she recognised ... a ship and a palace, a Spanish type of palace.

But she *could* establish words, and her mouth opened in disbelief, then closed in shame. Disbelief that she could have fetched the wrong man from the Hotel Stella, shame that she had said what she had about Macao, a *portuguese* settlement. She had said: 'Not nice.' She had said: 'Shady reputation.' She had said: 'Another sort of thing.' She had said *that*!

For the embroidered crest left her in no doubt at all about its wearer. He was Portuguese ... and something more than that: he was a *marques*. Clo was aware that even in these days Portuguese noblemen still existed, that they simply called themselves Senhor, but they still had all the trappings, even if these trappings were tucked away in their minds.

But this particular Marques, this Vincente de Velira (in very fine stitches), had it in more than his mind. It was on his elegant vest, his immaculate trunks, on his silk handkerchief that had fallen down as well. The cork tree, the ship, the *palacio*—for a *palacio* in this instance it would certainly be—all looked up and back at her. His name did.

'The Marques Vincente de Velira,' said Clo in a shocked voice.

At once the man on the floor stirred. He opened his dark eyes and looked up at Clo. When he spoke it was in the correct English he had used before.

'Yes?' he said. Then there was a pause ... a deliberate one?

'Yes—*senhorita*?' he asked.

CHAPTER TWO

'*Senhorita*?' Clo heard herself echoing foolishly—more, she thought, for something to say.

'Why not?' the man challenged. 'Already' ... a glance down at himself and the telltale crests ... 'you've established me as Portuguese.'

'Titled Portuguese,' Clo said bitterly, bitter at her embarrassing position. 'A grandee, no less.'

'Far less,' he assured her. 'Grandees go back to the Castilian days. I'm much humbler.'

'But still not just Mr.'

'In my work I'm never called anything but Senhor Velira,' he told her.

'But underneath?' She could not resist that.

'Underneath?'

'That embroidery.'

'That embroidery,' he said coldly, 'is the work of a tiresome aunt. Tia Juanita is one of the old school. Because she's old herself, I just go along.'

'She makes you wear those things?' asked Clo.

'Senhorita, no one makes me do anything.'

'There speaks a grandee!'

'There speaks Vincente Velira. If it pleases Dona——'

'Dona?' she queried.

'My aunt, the Dona Juanita del Carross——'

'Oh, all that again!'

He ignored Clo's interruption; he also deviated from the particular conversation. 'Would I be asking too much if I requested a robe?' he said. 'I'm not at all happy lying on exhibition like this.'

17

'But until the doctor comes——'

'No doctor,' broke in Ah Seng knowledgeably, 'no hurt to Master, only hurt to vase, vase all bloken. Finish.'

'She's right, you know,' the Portuguese came in, 'they always are. I'll probably have a headache later, but I'm perfectly sound, and I would like to get up.'

'Sit up would be more prudent in the beginning.'

'I said get up.'

'And no one tells you what to do,' nodded Clo.

'No one. Your hand, please. Yours, Amah.'

Both the women extended their hands, but it soon became obvious he needed more than that. For all his slimness, he was quite a heavy man. Clo was about to propose a pillow and a rug while she went out to enlist help when help came. It came through the door in the form of another tall male, casually, even a little untidily, dressed, rather tousle-haired, very tanned, freckled arms, big grin.

'What's going on? Why was I left at the Stella while you two—— Oh, heavens to Betsy!'

The newcomer had the victim up in a minute, relaxing in a chair in another minute, Clo in a second chair in a third minute, himself on the settee a moment later. Ah Seng was jollied out to bring in tea. 'Or something better if you have any,' the man hinted.

Then the new professor, the real professor, turned to Clo and introduced: 'Harry Ferrier—you might have heard of me.'

'Of course,' she smiled. 'Applied Pacific Sciences.'

'Spot on. I was waiting as directed at the Stella for you, but you never came.'

'I did, though.'

'I can see that now. You came and preferred Milord.'

'Marques,' corrected Senhor Velira deliberately and with a sidelong glance at Clo, 'but Milord will be accepted. Anything but a grandee.'

'Good old Vincente!' The Australian grinned at him, grinned quite affectionately. 'Even though I was passed over I'm glad you two have met.'

'I can't share your pleasure, Harry,' the Marques protested. 'I've just been cut out of a very good suit.'

'It was an emergency,' pleaded Clo, 'and I shall pay for the damage, of course.'

'I wouldn't be too rash,' Harry Ferrier warned Clo. 'Vincente does have expensive taste.'

'I shall still pay.'

'Certainly,' the Marques accepted.

That silenced Clo, but it appeared to break up Harry Ferrier. He fairly exploded into delighted guffaws, and only the sight of Ah Seng bearing a tray sobered him.

'Jasmine tea,' presented Clo blandly, finding her tongue again, 'much better than beer.'

This time it was the Portuguese who laughed. He laughed at Harry, and under cover of the laughter Clo slipped out to tidy herself.

As she ran the comb through her acorn hair in their neighbouring family unit, she saw through the window her father coming along to the hall of residence, and for a moment she held the comb aloft in surprise. Why, she thought, he seems quite old; Dad is looking like an old man today. She stood silent a while, then finished herself off with a pink lipstick and a touch of turquoise eye-shadow.

When she went back to the flats, her father was there, too, and he looked younger again.

Dad must have rustled up some beer from somewhere, and they were all drinking it, Harry Ferrier and Dad who hailed from a beer country, and the grandee ... again Clo found herself calling him that ... who surely preferred something much more genteel.

But everyone looked happy enough ... except Ah Seng. Ah Seng was bearing out the untouched jasmine tea and grumbling about the vase again. 'Finish,' she muttered, 'all gone. Bloken.'

'*Senhorita*.' The Marques was offering Clo a glass of the beer. She accepted it, eyes down like the demure girls in the street, but only, like the demure girls again, those eyes down after a fleeting glance.

The fleeting glance met his glance, dark but with a red fire somewhere, and not fleeting. His black lashes gave the merest flick.

Clo closed herself in silence, which was easy in the animated male talk, especially Harry Ferrier's robust variety; she let the words drift round her. What an utter fool she had been, and what an utter fool he must think her, not only collecting a wrong man, but saying what she had, and, worst of all, doing what she did.

She became conscious that the conversation had come round to that, or rather to the condition now of Senhor Velira's suit.

'You'll have to borrow something of mine,' Harry Ferrier was saying, 'you can't go back on the Star Ferry wrapped up in a rug.'

'I'll accept your offer,' the Marques agreed. 'If I were proceeding to the house on the hill' . . . what house? Clo wondered, what hill? . . . 'you could drive me, but I'm staying at the Stella until Tia returns with Isabella, and transporting me to Kowloon by way of the tunnel would be a sacrilege in magic weather like this.' He glanced at the blue and gold perfection of the day through the unit window.

'Aunt away so stopping at the pub, eh?' criticised Harry goodnaturedly. 'Can't boil yourself an egg?'

'My aunt evidently believes not, for she ordered the house to be closed. When I returned I was literally shut out.'

'Yet no one tells you what to do.' Clo heard herself inserting that pertly, and drew an apprehensive breath.

The Portuguese turned dark, unrevealing eyes on Clo. 'It's my aunt's residence,' he said.

He waited a moment, then resumed: 'Even though this eastern corner of the world is her headquarters, her late husband having conducted his various businesses here, Tia Juanita will not live in our own Portuguese Macao, she has this quaint idea ... along with others ... that it's not "nice", that it has a bad reputation, that sort of thing.' He turned his head now and looked fully at Clo.

Clo did not answer back.

'I'll have to see this Macao,' came in Harry, intrigued, 'play some fan-tan, win myself some pretty Portuguese girl.'

This time the *senhor* did not stiffen. He smiled back at Harry and actually winked at him. A wink from a *marques*!

'Alas, Macao is all that, or so Tia Juanita ... and others ... say, yet it's more things, sweet, elusive things, as well. It's all summer in your hand as you sip Portuguese wine in the Posado de Macao on a calm afternoon, as you drift off to sleep to the whirr of little insects, to the twitter of bulbul birds, to the clop of wooden pattens. Then there are the Baroque churches, the allure of the Street of Eternal Felicity.'

'That sounds wonderful.' Despite herself Clo had to break in. For all her years here she had never visited Macao, and the street name charmed her.

'Ah, but it's not "nice",' he reminded her suavely.

Clo's discomposure was broken by Ah Seng's reappearance and her triumphant presentation of Second Son, Tang. Amah had evidently gone out, called him and scrubbed him up, for drops of water still shone on his close cap of hair and roses from a hard brush stained his gold cheeks. He looked good enough to eat, Clo thought with a glow of her own. Clo loved all these Cantonese children, but Tang ...

well, Tang in any country, any language, was special.

He was bullet-headed as usual, and a customary deep gold, but more a deep sunflower gold. Clo always thought of him as a sunflower spirit not a small Cantonese. He had a forest of very long, very thick lashes, and when at last you glimpsed the eyes behind the lashes you did not find the expected alert, rather gamin child eyes, you found castle-building eyes, cloudland eyes, man-in-the-moon eyes, the eyes of a little boy deep in dreams.

He was intelligent, but, unlike his mother who had had more exposure, he spoke no English; Ah Seng reported that he did his lessons very well, but obviously he lived in a private world for when you spoke to him he seemed to emerge from a long way off. He would be a poet, thought Clo, or an artist, or——

Clo felt eyes on her, and turned and met the dark eyes of the Senhor. She took her own glance away at once, but not before she received an unexpected impression. The impression that the Marques de Velira was smiling ... gently ... at her.

'Ah Seng,' she scolded at once, 'what are you doing?' For Amah, doubtless having heard the Senhor's agreement to borrow Harry Ferrier's clothes, and wishing to be helpful, was tumbling the contents of the young professor's rather shabby bag all over the floor. It was inevitable, Clo supposed, that a pair of plain, cotton, *un*crested trunks came out on top, bringing everything back again.

'Return them at once,' Clo ordered.

'No,' counter-ordered the Marques, 'leave out that and that and that. And now, if I can impose on you, I'll change, Harry, and return to the mainland.'

'Accompanied by Clo,' insisted Doctor Denning. '*Yes*, Clo. You got Vincente' ... Vincente already! ... 'into this, now you'll see it through.'

'Mr Velira already knows Hong Kong, Dad,' Clo told him.

'Vincente has suffered a head injury and might still receive a delayed concussion. No, Clo, *you* will see him home. Anyway, I don't want you around here. Harry and I, as can be expected, have a lot to say to each other.'

Clo had a lot, too, but absolutely no chance of saying it. She watched sulkily as the Marques rose and retired discreetly beneath the concealing rug to Harry's bedroom, watched sulkily as he returned, got up sulkily and preceded him sulkily out and down.

'Don't,' the Marques advised in an un-Portuguese manner, 'trip over your bottom lip or we'll both be running the risk of concussion.'

'The boat is in,' Clo snapped back, and she led the way to the wharf, hoping that this time it was not the same gamin boy as before.

It was not, and they took a seat and watched the ferry pull out.

'I'm sorry.' It cost Clo dearly, but in all fairness she knew she had to say it.

'I'm not,' he returned, promptly and apparently with sincerity. 'It's been fun. Why does the English race seem to have such a claim on that?'

'On fun?'

'Yes.'

'Don't Portuguese?' she asked.

'My cousin Isabella has, but then she was English-schooled.' A sigh. 'Frankly, I'm apprehensive for Isabella.'

He proceeded to tell Clo, tell her simply, no gossip, no chit-chat, an account as to why he was uneasy about his cousin.

'Isabella is young, beautiful and a widow,' he began.

'Very sad,' said Clo, a little puzzled, puzzled that this very self-sufficient man was speaking like this to her.

He must have heard the puzzled note, for he explained at once: 'You are the same age, and that's why I'm telling you this. I know no other young girls to speak to about Isabella.'

'You must know many,' Clo disbelieved.

'Lovely young women, yes, but not grown-up children. I'm sorry if that offends you.'

'It doesn't, it flatters me, but you're wrong—I'm rising twenty-one.'

'So young!' he commented.

'As young as Isabella?'

'The same. The young Condessa is also twenty, and please not to remark "Oh, all that again!" We can't help our rank—the males, anyway.'

'The female doesn't inherit?'

'Only if there's no male heir. But Isabella's parents, anyway, had no rank to pass on.'

'Yet she is titled? You said Condessa?'

'Through marriage, the same as it was once with Tia Juanita, in fact I often suspect——'

'Yes, senhor?'

'I often think it persuaded Tia to push Isabella.'

'Into marriage?'

'Yes.'

'Then some Portuguese are told what to do?'

'Touché.' He smiled at Clo. 'Even I am told by Tia.'

'Crests on your underthings?'

'Alas, yes.'

'She wouldn't know if you didn't wear them,' Clo pointed out.

'When you meet Tia Juanita ... oh, yes, you will meet her, I've thought of something ... you'll know differently. She has sharp black eyes that see everything, she knows everything.'

... He had thought of something. Clo puzzled over that

for a moment, then decided it was beyond her.

'Senhor Velira,' she asked, 'why are you recounting all this?'

'You find it uninteresting?'

'On the contrary. But what is it you want to know?'

'To tell, not know. Though I shall be grateful for an answer later.'

'Answer? Later?'

'As to what you think of Isabella.'

'Your cousin.'

'My dead mother's late sister's daughter. Yes. Isabella's mamma died, too. Isabella was English-schooled.' He said it again.

'As you were?'

'Partly. I also went to Paris. America. Lately to Australia to study——'

'Applied Pacific Sciences?'

'Yes. There I met Harry. We roomed together.'

'That must have been a trial,' commented Clo. 'He seems untidy.'

'He was untidy and it was a trial, but at once we were friends, and one forgives anything in a friend. At least...' He was looking deeply at Clo, looking in a way she did not comprehend, and the depth of the look made her cheeks grow hot.

'At least, *almost* anything,' he amended.

'Yes, *senhor*?' Clo prompted. 'You were telling me about Isabella?'

'Tia Juanita imagined Isabella in a cloistered English school, eyes on her books, very docile, very sweet. But Isabella—well——'

'A rebel?'

'Not exactly, but with a definite taste for life. Nonetheless when the marriage was arranged for her——'

'Oh, no!' gasped Clo indignantly.

'Let me finish, please ... she readily agreed. She was young, and flattered to be wed so early, years probably before her school contemporaries. Had she not agreed so wholeheartedly I would have stepped in.'

'You, Marques?'

'Indeed, *senhorita*. I might endure crests on undershirts, but I would not abide *that*. She married this nobleman with wide-open eyes. He died soon after. He was a very old, very titled, very rich man. The riches, of course, will come in time to Isabella, and the title has already, so long as she does not remarry.'

'I think I begin to see light. Your Tia Juanita wishes Isabella to retain her rank and not remarry.'

'In all fairness,' the Senhor shrugged wryly, 'Tia would have no objection to a higher rank, even an equal one. But a lesser rank, or no rank at all? No way.' The slang on his elegant lips amused Clo, and she had to laugh. Presently he laughed as well.

'Well, *senhorita*?' he asked at last.

'Should she or shouldn't she remarry, you mean?'

'If the opportunity presents itself, yes, that is my question.'

'Well, she should marry again, decidedly, but why ... oh, why did she in the first place?'

'Marry a man she did not love? You mean you wouldn't?'

'Not for all the grandees in the world, not for all the riches,' said Clo earnestly.

'I see. Then what would win you?'

'Just love, I guess.'

'Nothing else?'

'Just love, *senhor*.'

'But what is love, *senhorita*?'

'In Portuguese?'

'You speak the language?'

'I meant in Portuguese thinking.'

'What would you know about Portuguese thinking?'

'A little—now.'

'Now?' he queried.

'Back in the residence hall.' Clo more stammered than said it.

'Yes?'

'Macao—what you told me. Drifting off to sleep to the whirr of little insects ... the twitter of the bulbul birds ... the clop of wooden pattens. All summer in your hand.'

'Time,' he agreed in a soft voice, 'standing still. Thank you, *senhorita*. I think you're telling me you are a little disappointed in Isabella, as I was, but that she was young, is still young, and that next time she must marry for love.'

'Did I say all that?' Clo smiled.

The Star Ferry was midway across, Kowloon the raffish before them, Victoria Hong Kong side with its Peak above it behind. Peak! Hill! The house on the hill!

'Your aunt's house is up there?' Clo asked.

'Yes.' He could not resist adding remindingly: 'Instead of shady Macao.'

Clo said eagerly, eager to make amends: 'It's very lovely on the Peak. The ferries look like little gold bugs at night. It's perfect to watch festivals.'

'I'm strictly a business man, little time for festivals,' he said. 'Tell me about some.'

'The Moon Festival,' Clo began, 'when people look up to be the first to see the hare who sits in the moon, the Bun Festival, that's on Cheung Chau Island, which finishes in pyramids of pink sugar cakes. But you'll see the best of all this year if you're here.'

'Oh, yes.' His voice came very decisive, very clear, absolutely certain. 'I shall be here. But why this year, *senhorita*?'

'Because it's the Year of the Dragon, and dragons are the most exciting of all.'

'All what?'

The other years—rat, ox, tiger, hare, dragon, snake, goat, horse, monkey, cock, dog and pig. Dragons puff out smoke, they turn into princes, they do dream things. I believed that, anyway, when I turned nine. That was my first Year of the Dragon, this is my second. I remember that the streets were full of lanterns, crackers, there were lion dancers, and I was given a paper bird on a string.'

'You sound,' the Marques teased, 'like young Tang looked.'

Clo turned to him in surprise. 'You felt that, too?' she asked. 'Kind of folded in dreams?'

'Yes.'

'I always think of Tang as a sunflower spirit, not a little boy.' Clo sat silent a while, musing.

He broke into her thoughts. 'I believe he is made of stardust,' he agreed.

The ferry was pulling in.

'You will not alight with me,' the Marques commanded, 'you've done enough.'

'Is that good or bad?' Clo asked.

'You've atoned,' he altered. 'Thank you for your advice.'

'But I gave none.'

'I received some.'

'You are—odd,' she said curiously.

'Is that good or bad?'

'It's—different,' Clo said.

'Splendid. I will need difference. I will need everything I can muster, I believe.'

'What do you mean, *senhor*?'

'Harry is a very attractive young man. You find him so?'

'I've barely met him.'

'But when you do?'

'I won't like him. How can I?' she sighed. 'He's to take my father's place.'

'He will take it well.'

'But take it.'

The Portuguese paused, as though to say something, but must have changed his mind.

'*Bom dias*, Senhorita Denning.' The tall, elegant man moved away. But after a few steps he turned round again.

'*Clo*—what is that short for, *senhorita*?' he asked, puzzled.

'Clotilda, in French meaning a fighting woman, in English a green shoot.'

'I choose the green shoot, and yet' ... appraisingly ... 'I do not know. A fighting woman? yes, perhaps.'

'I know the name of Vincente,' Clo retorted promptly, 'it means Conquering.'

'So,' he said, and he tapped the tips of his long fingers together and looked fully at her. He looked a long time.

'*Bom dias*, Marques de Velira,' Clo called wickedly, and she made a hurried but deliberate curtsey ... then a strategic retreat.

Back at the residence hall again, Harry Ferrier pounced on her as she tried to pass his door to gain their own flat.

'These communal corridors!' Clo grumbled, fairly caught on her toes as she tried to sneak by.

'What's wrong with me?' Harry Ferrier demanded. 'The pox?'

'Nothing's wrong. You are, I am assured by the Portuguese nobility, untidy but nice.'

'Come in and see,' he enticed.

'Are you trying to pick me up?' Clo asked boldly.

'Lickshaw, lady? Lickshaw? Velly nice digs, velly nice Australian gentleman. I show?'

'You win,' sighed Clo. 'I'll come.' She went in.

Amah had fetched another vase, Clo's favourite china red one. The Australian had dumped ... you could only call it that ... a sad geranium in it.

'It's for looking,' Clo protested, 'not for holding plants. Didn't you know?'

'I need a wife,' he excused himself.

'Lickshaw men don't generally go in for that side,' Clo retorted.

'Hear my reason, kind lady. I'm an orphan.'

'Orphans stop being orphans at eighteen, and you're more than that,' she smiled.

'Then I'm an orphan emeritus.'

'Yes, Professor Ferrier,' Clo indulged.

'Seriously,' he said with a maddeningly winning smile, 'I've never had a home or family, only homes and families. I'd like to begin now.'

'I think,' Clo retorted wisely, 'you only want a bigger flat—the bachelor digs are rather meagre.'

He grinned and she grinned back. It was not a very good start to hating, she thought.

Harry Ferrier got busy at the buffet and presently returned with two glasses of wine.

'You've discovered *shau shing* already!' *Shau shing* was the local rice wine.

'Yes, also the salute: *Yam seng*—bottoms up.'

'It should be drunk from a small cup,' Clo told him, 'but never mind.'

He drained the rice wine. 'Is that your policy? Never mind?'

'I try not to mind.' All the same Clo had to bite her lip.

'You mean your father out, me in?'

'Yes.'

'It had to happen, you know.' He smiled apologetically at her, and he had the nicest gold-brown eyes. 'Yes,' he nodded, watching Clo, 'I've been told they're like a dog's.'

He was irresistible. Somewhere in the space of five minutes Clo gave up trying to resist him.

'The Marques thinks a lot of you,' she told him.

'I think the world of Vince,' he assured her.

'What part of the world? Portugal?'

'You're pumping me as to what part is his part. It's all places—here, there, everywhere. He's an economic globe-trotter. That's how I met him in Sydney. But this, fair lady, is *my* very first journey abroad.'

'You're thrilled?'

'To the back teeth. Oh, I'm sorry for you, but it's still so.' He looked rueful.

'That's all right, you can't help it, if it hadn't been you it would have been someone else. Did—did Dad say when?'

'D-Day?'

'Yes.'

'Oh, ages yet. You see, I've got it all here in theory.' Harry tapped his head. 'But I have to cram in twenty years of practical from the good doctor.'

'How long will that take?'

'I'm a slow learner,' he shrugged.

'You know I didn't mean that, you know I meant—Dad. Dad must have given you some indication in your talk today.'

A pause, a pause so moth-winged it might not have been a pause at all.

'Not a clue,' Harry Ferrier smiled. 'Another *shau shing*?'

'Certainly not, and you shouldn't either after beer.'

'How long,' he disbelieved, 'since you've been to Australia?'

'Not long enough, going by you.'

'Will you, Clotilda?'

'Will I what?'

'Go by me.'

'Oh, for heaven's sake, what a man!' she sighed. 'I've had enough of you. I'm going to leave you to Ah Seng's tender mercies.'

'How tender?'

'Triumphant daily reports of her market cunning on your behalf, intimate displays of her shopping for each meal, every article held up for you to admire her frugality, chickens shoved at you, ducks, dead fish with reproachful eyes.'

'I can't wait,' he grinned. 'And the end result?'

'Mouth-watering. She cooks wonderful Chinese dinners.'

'... And others?'

'Why do you think I'm an unemployed female? My father keeps me home particularly to cook lamb.'

'Thanks for the hint. No lamb. Unless, of course, I'm invited out.' He looked meaningly at Clo. 'But' ... before she could shake a head or nod ... 'I know all about that unemployment of yours. You're a tower of strength here. You're just what a residence hall of men need.'

'That could have been put better,' she smiled.

'You're needed to be around with a needle and thread,' he ignored her, 'to collect new innocents from the Hotel Stella, see to roast lamb, all that. I think your father was a very wise man.'

'He didn't do it for that, he did it because, in spite of every encouragement from every lecturer, I didn't make university grades, only college corridor ones.'

'Suits me.'

'It wasn't intended to.'

They went on and on in happy argument. Ah Seng, fearing a quarrel, put her head round the door in concern, found Clo sitting on the table swinging her legs as she thought of outrageous things to say, found new master lying on the settee and giving back as good as he got. Everyone happy.

To welcome happy new master she would *not* serve him that young chicken stuffed with ginger, chestnuts, lotus seed, olives and little pink mushrooms after all; she would hurry out and buy some—lamb.

CHAPTER THREE

For the rest of that week Clo saw nothing of her new male acquaintance.

She did not know where the Marques was ... still at the Hotel Stella? around the world on some new trade mission? up at the house on the Peak with his aunt and cousin?

Harry Ferrier was still on hand, though, for she could hear him through the thin hall of residence walls, indeed, she could follow every word. Man-like he was trying to show Ah Seng how she wasted her energy. They all did that in the beginning. It was a waste of *his* energy, Clo could have told Harry. Drying racks for dishes, blenders, all labour-savers were looked upon with deep suspicion by these wonderful helpers. Everything was done the old, laborious way. On the other hand, Clo also could have told Harry that overworked-looking Amah did not really exert herself as much as it appeared, she just plodded along. Also what would she have done with spare time? Only found some other old laborious chore.

Clo filled in her days as she always had filled them, shopping for the college staff for the things they preferred not to leave to a Cantonese housekeeper. Stamps, a scarf or a cheongsam or a pair of silk pyjamas to send to a favourite niece, books to be picked up, toiletries.

Dad gave Clo a good report on Harry.

'He's right,' he said, well pleased.

'You mean he'll be able to fill your shoes in time.'

'Any time. Clo, he just won his audience at once. That's hard, you know.'

Clo did know. Her father often had been discouraged

33

about student reaction, they had not smiled when he had played for smiles, sometimes they had laughed where no laughs were called for. But years of experience had taught the Doctor that these dedicated young men and women approached learning much more seriously than in the West, that smiles were often considered to be flippant, that unexpected laughter on their part was often a cover-up for emotion, which of course must be controlled, for at heart they were very emotional and easily stirred.

When Clo did run into Harry Ferrier at last she was pleased to see he had realised all this, and that he appreciated it.

'I had to work hard for my education myself ... that poor orphan, you know ... so I understand those dedicated young ladies in their innocent little girl smocks over their seductive cheongsams, those dedicated young men all spectacles and eagerness, but Clo, Clo, when do they go boom?'

'What, Harry?'

'Boom. When do they protest, object, argue, interrupt, interrogate, correct a point?'

'Do they in Australia?'

'All countries. Why, students *burst*.'

'Here it's a great honour to go to higher learning,' she told him. 'All the students' parents would have deprived themselves. The boys and girls are aware of that and are very determined to succeed.'

'Good luck to them, then, but it's harder on me.'

'You like arguments? You're an aggressive Australian?'

'So you've heard of that!' he grinned. 'No, the reason is I have to keep my nose to the grindstone to keep a chapter ahead of them. I badly need some relaxation. How about it, Clo?'

'How about what?'

'Showing this poor bloke around. I want to see and hear and taste Hong Kong.'

Clo agreed, for she was as keen as he was, even after twenty years. As a holiday was approaching ... English holidays were celebrated as well as Chinese festivals ... and compulsory stand-down for the college occurring, they decided to use it and to start early and fill every hour.

Harry had a list of what he wanted to do. Bath-house ... Clo grinned secretly at that, knowing that what Harry anticipated and what he would get would be two different things ... Repulse Bay or some other beach location for a swim, Aberdeen for a floating restaurant lunch, then, joy of joys, shopping. 'Without buying anything,' Harry added. 'I haven't a bean.'

'Who will pay for your bath?' she asked. 'Pay for the fish you choose to be cooked?'

'*My* bath ... isn't it one of those glamorous community affairs?'

'Wrong country. You're thinking of Japan. It's a plain tub here in a single, rather hospital-looking bathroom.'

'Rule that out, then, and rule out the floating restaurant. I'd feel a murderer choosing a certain fish.'

'You might choose it, but you wouldn't get it,' she assured him. 'Something happens in the kitchen. Anyway, if you went again the next day, your fish, had you tagged it, would still be swimming around. I vote we settle for the sea and sun. We'll take our togs and have a fine time under the watchful eye of the "swim-swim" boys. Only if you're drowning, Harry, don't start babbling "Save me", because most of the "swim-swim" boys don't know any English.'

'Lunch?'

'We can buy *deem-sum* and *chow-fan* as we walk along.'

'Clotilda, you're a wizard!' he grinned.

'You called me Clotilda before. Who told you?'—A fighting woman, she had offered the Marques, or a green shoot.

'I asked your father. After all, I have to have your name

correct when I apply for our marriage licence.'

'Oh, Harry, you are a fool!' she smiled.

'A nice fool?'

'Well—yes.'

'A nice fool from you will do me for starters. When will we start off?'

They started off early on the stand-down morning, both in comfortable, slightly shabby clothes, which Clo said would be more suitable for the mixed day they planned. She was to regret that later.

Harry, having found out about the bath-house, decided to forgo the experience, especially when Clo related with relish that the bath boys, or so she had been told, really scoured and scrubbed.

'I had enough of that in my deprived childhood,' Harry grimaced. 'There was one housemother who was obsessed with ingrained dirt. She declared that all boys harboured ingrained dirt.'

They decided, too, to eliminate the floating restaurant, in case the fish they chose *did* get served up to them and they felt too sad to eat. A snack here and there would do. Leaving, Clo said, a swim and a bargain hunt.

It was a perfect day for bathing, hot enough to entice you to hurry to the cool green water, cool enough not to enervate you by the time you reached there.

They changed at a waterside hotel and went down to a crescent of sand rimming a rippling bay.

As at most of the beaches, a raft floated in the middle of the bathing area with a 'swim-swim' boy on the raft to keep an eye out for anyone in difficulty. He wore a round red straw hat and he smiled continually. As he didn't speak English, Clo again warned Harry if he found himself suddenly sinking not to call 'Save me' but to scream. Screams were known in every language.

'And you, Clo?'

'I'll do the Australian crawl.'

'After twenty years!'

'I thought it came naturally,' she teased.

'I'm coming after you naturally.' For Clo had plunged in and started to swim off. With swift, experienced strokes Harry followed her.

They clowned around, splashing water at each other, taking turns to dive between each other's legs, performing small swimming tricks they thought they did rather well, then Harry turned on his stomach for some serious laps, and Clo turned on her back for a luxurious float.

The sun danced on the water and danced on Clo's eyes. To avoid the glare, she closed her eyes, gave herself up to the sheer delight of idle, sleepy drifting.

She could not have said at what juncture full consciousness returned, or what alerted her; perhaps a small change in the temperature, or the beach voices that had been musically distant before, no longer audible at all.

She trod water and looked round. Heavens, she couldn't have drifted this far!

But she had, and she had better swim, not drift, back. She struck out.

Ordinarily she would have had no difficulty, she was a safe if unspectacular swimmer, but it was the season of jellyfish, and though there was no grave danger from them, a sting could be very painful, could last for hours. Clo knew this because she had suffered before, so now she tried to avoid the large, heart-like, quivering shapes with their strings of stinging tentacles, but, because out here in deeper, less crowded water the jellyfish were more profuse, she had to swim a longer distance than she should have swum. She started to get tired.

Wisely she trod water again and looked around. To her relief she saw Harry, and saw that he had seen her. She saw him starting across. But someone else was coming, too, the last person in Hong Kong Clo had expected to see swimming, though no doubt the Portuguese bathed in the sea, and no doubt a *marques* did as well. It was Senhor Velira. A little hysterically, but killing the hysteria at once, for lack of self-control was the last thing one wanted in a situation like this, Clo wondered if there was a cork tree, a ship and a *palacio* embroidered on his swimming briefs.

Neither man had seen the other, both were eating up the distance with long, strong strokes. What, Clo wondered, was the Portuguese equivalent of an Australian crawl? But more pressing than that, what was she to do? Both would hate arriving to 'save' her at the same time. They would feel idiots, and she would feel——

Clo could only think of one thing, so she did it. She dived right under, stayed there, came up spluttering and seeing to it that she caught the 'swim-swim' boy's eye.

Almost in a second, for the raft was much closer than either of the men, the boy was beside Clo and supporting her. He side-stroked her to his raft and helped her up. He looked very pleased with himself. His employer would be pleased, and no doubt there would be *tippu*. He replaced his round red hat and beamed at Clo, who beamed back.

The two men, seeing what had happened, changed direction and instead swam to the raft. Between them Clo returned to the beach. Nothing was said, no comment was made, for which Clo was very thankful.

After dressing at the hotel, she sought out the manager to give him a reward for the 'swim-swim' boy.

'Already,' smiled the manager.

'Already? But——'

'The gentleman.'

'There were two——' Clo stopped. One of the gentlemen had been broke, Harry had. When she went out to the patio, Harry and Vincente were waiting for her, and she said stiffly to the Marques: 'Thank you, but I would have attended to that myself.'

'To what, *senhorita*?'

'*Tippu*. A thank-you to the "swim-swim" boy.'

'Oh, I was aware of that. I just handed a few notes over while the manager was around in case you forgot.'

'I don't forget,' she assured him.

'The matter of a suit?'

'I haven't forgotten that—Harry, stop guffawing!'

They got into stride together and walked beside the water. Had they lunched yet? the Marques inquired.

In Australia, Harry explained, lunch came *after* swimming, not before, in case you sank.

'*You* certainly would,' Clo said crossly, 'there's never been so much food taken into the hall of residence since you arrived.'

'Now we're both getting it,' the Marques smiled to Harry. 'An empty stomach, would you say? or delayed reaction?'

'This female specimen has nerves of steel, Vince.' Harry touched Clo's shoulder and she shook him off. 'Where's that *deem-sum* shop you told me about, Clo?'

'*Deem-sum!*' It was the Marques. 'Oh, no!'

'Also *chow-fan*.'

'No again, we must have a proper dinner, my friends.'

'But——'

'And I know just the place.' Without giving them time to demur, and Harry obviously had no intention of demurring, Vincente led them down tht promenade to a smaller hotel than the other glittering palaces, yet quiet, expensive-looking and in very good taste. The Marques said: 'I know this place.'

The other two would have been aware of that without him telling them so; these hotels always received you with deference, but for the Marques now the red carpet was unrolled. Not literally, of course, for the interior was tropically furnished, bare shining floors, much bamboo, filtered sunlight. But the service was excellent plus, it made Clo feel a queen ... except for her clothes. A queen in denim, she thought. Why hadn't she worn something else?

However, dress wasn't bothering Harry, so she did not let it bother her. She was hungry after her swim, and even if she hadn't been the setting of the table would have enticed her. Round, as Chinese eating-out tables generally are, exquisitely appointed—individual small bowls, wrapped chopsticks, dishes of waiting sauces, oyster, soya, sesame. Hot towels sprinkled with rosewater to dab at your face and hands before and after eating. Hovering waiters setting wonderful food down in the middle of the table for the guests to help themselves, as was always done here. They never ... annoyingly ... stood around.

Something else was always done, which Clo knew, and probably the Marques knew, but possibly Harry didn't. The gentleman served the lady on his right, making a big show of choosing the choicest morsels for her. And the lady? She had to protest. Too much! Too, *too* much! Please, only a fragment. Clo, ravenous, did so ... then burst into laughter. The Marques joined her, then they explained to a bewildered Harry what was taking place.

'But to do it properly,' Harry said, 'there should be a fourth, Vincente.'

'Yes, indeed ... and I think I see the very one.'

The Senhor had risen, excused himself and left them. It was not very long before he returned. With him was an extremely elegant woman, older than Clo, mid-twenties, Clo judged, flawlessly turned-out, flawlessly made-up, attractive, graceful, stylish. In Harry's slang, and for Clo's ear only: 'Big deal.'

'Senhorita Martinez,' bowed the Marques, 'may I present Miss Clotilda Denning, the daughter of Doctor Denning, and Harry Ferrier, the new professor. Miss Denning, Harry, may I present Senhorita Aviella Martinez, a niece, on Tia's husband's side, of Dona Juanita, and resident, when the mood takes her as it has taken her now, of Hong Kong. Is that right, distant cousin?' He smiled at Aviella.

Aviella Martinez pouted prettily and complained: 'Distant, Vincente?'

'Actually no relation at all.'

'... Well, perhaps it's all the better for that.' Now the smile was provocative. Aviella turned to Harry. 'A professor,' she considered. For the merest moment her lovely dark eyes took in Harry, then his crumpled slacks, his open-neck shirt ... *particularly* these, Clo thought.

Mere though the glance was, Harry must have seen the look as well as Clo. 'Mufti,' he explained. 'Gowns and mortarboards are not my cup of tea.'

'Cup of tea?' she queried.

'I like to be free,' he explained.

'Oh.' Now the gaze was on Clo, denim Clo, white schoolgirlish blouse. What had Clo to use for an excuse?

'We've all been swimming,' Clo stammered.

'All? Not you, too, Vincente?'

'Yes, my dear. Did you think I could not swim?'

'Oh, I know you can, but——'

'But?'

'On the beach, Vincente?'

'Where else?'

'Your hotel pool, of course.'

'On the beach. Now, down to business. We are hungry. But for Harry's instructions we are doing the thing in the proper Cantonese style, and we need another fair lady to be pressed to eat.'

'Really, Vincente, I don't think I'm hungry.'

'Then that is excellent, for the role of the lady is to pretend a delicate appetite, to protest at being served too much. When you protest, we can believe you ... not like someone else we know.'

'I can second that,' laughed Harry. 'Clo here can eat a

horse. I say, she's not eating one, is she?'

'Pork,' said the Marques, 'with pineapple, mandarin and egg noodles. All right, Professor Ferrier, prevail upon the lady on your right, which is Senhorita Martinez, to partake.'

'You have the easier job,' Harry grumbled, 'but I' ... brightening ... 'seeing Senhorita Martinez is not hungry, will get the biggest plate.'

Clo felt that she was not hungry any longer either; one look at those fashionable, impeccable clothes had dismayed her. 'No more,' she said to the Marques, and her voice actually cracked.

'It's only a pretended refusal,' he said softly to her, 'you don't have to take it to heart.'

'I—I look awful.'

'Yes.'

'Denim——' she protested.

'It certainly isn't silk,' he agreed.

'You shouldn't have brought us here.'

'Be quiet, Miss Denning, and drink your rice wine. That might make you feel a little more confident.' He poured the *shaushing* that had arrived, then held up in his small porcelain cup, toasting. *'Yam seng.'*

'Yes,' seconded Harry, 'bottoms up.'

Senhorita Martinez gave a barely perceptible movement of her very beautiful shoulders in the straw silk dress. The wine relaxed her, though, just as it relaxed Clo. Clo forgot her denim, forgot the custom of protesting at being served too much, and simply tucked in.

'So Dona Juanita and Isabella are expected back,' Senhorita Martinez said to Vincente over jasmine tea.

'Yes. Tomorrow.'

'Poor child,' sighed Aviella, 'such sorrow for one so young. She will remain some time in mourning?'

'No, she will not.'

'Are you serious, Vincente?'

'About that I am adamant. I am Portuguese, yes, but not all things Portuguese are perfect.'

The Senhorita pouted, and the gallant Senhor hastened to say: 'That does not include you, Aviella.'

Aviella Martinez smiled again, but said she was not sure about these new relaxed attitudes.

'You should be, he told her. 'You, too, were English-schooled.'

'The same school as Isabella.'

'But before her.' This brought another pout, but this time the Marques did not exert himself to be gallant.

Aviella, seeing her whims were not being noticed, said: 'The young widow will need someone younger with her, someone younger than Dona Juanita.'

'That, too, occurred to me.'

'Then, Vincente, I am more than willing. I am senior to little Isabella, of course, but only by a few years. Dona Juanita is my father's brother's widow, she is my *tia* as well as yours, so she would be pleased to have me.' Aviella smiled blandly. 'I will go tomorrow.'

'It is only tomorrow they arrive, Aviella.'

'Then the day after.'

'No, I think not.'

'Vincente——'

'I have spoken, please. More wine, anyone? More tea? Then we will rise.'

Out on the steps Aviella asked: 'Why are you here, Vincente?'

'Business.'

'At the side of the sea?'

'Business is done here too, but, you must agree, more pleasantly. And you?'

'I am staying at the Repulse Bay Hotel for several days, I felt I needed the air.'

'You may have then, but you do not need it now, you need nothing, you are a flower.'

'Vincente, there is just no one like you for saying nice things,' Aviella smiled.

'True things.'

'Then why can't I——'

'*Bom dias*, Aviella,' he said firmly.

After they had left the very elegant Portuguese lady, after they had walked about a hundred yards, Clo asked curiously:

'Why?'

She asked it of Vincente.

'Why what, Clotilda?' he frowned.

'Why can't she go up and keep Isabella company?'

'It is Isabella's prerogative to choose her own company.'

'She might choose Aviella,' Clo pointed out.

'She would not.'

'You sound very knowledgeable, you sound as though you know whom she would choose.'

'I think I do.'

'Then there's Dona Juanita,' Clo persisted. 'She would have her say.'

'Why?'

'She's Isabella's guardian.'

'Guardian of a grown woman? A widow?'

'Well, it's Dona Juanita's house,' said Clo reasonably.

'It is not.'

'You said——'

'Oh, yes, I said, but I thought you would understand.'

'Understand what?'

'That it is hers, but only through my grace and favour.'

'Your what?' she queried.

'Grace and favour. You've heard of that surely.'

'Oh, yes, but——'

'Then it is mine in actuality, but Tia's for her own use. Understood?'

'Not entirely.'

'Then do not mind. I simply did not agree to Aviella because she is not what I have in mind for my cousin.'

'No?'

'No,' he said, and his black eyes with the fire in them fairly snapped.

'Then may I ask whom?'

'You may not ... but I have no doubt you will discover in a short time.'

'Discover?' questioned Clo.

'Discover is what I said. And now are you two ready to be delivered home? I have my car at hand.'

'No.' Both Harry and Clo said it in unison. 'We want to go shopping.'

'In some quiet and elegant store? Then I will come.'

'No, some crowded market place where we can bargain,' said Clo firmly.

'Then I leave you. I have no liking for such places. Shop well, and watch your wallets.' He shook Harry's hand, then turned to Clo. To her complete surprise, for though he had done it to Aviella, Aviella had looked the part, and Clo only looked everyday denim, he took and kissed her hand. Then he left.

For quite a while Clo could not speak. Harry was chattering excitedly, all this was new and strange and stimulating to him, but Clo could find no words. Her right hand kept feeling for her left hand, feeling the spot where he had brushed his lips. There was a little burn there, an oddly pleasant one. She kept touching the place until Harry noticed.

'You have to wash it off some time,' he said drily.

'Oh, Harry, I'm sorry, it was just—well, I've never had that done to me before.'

'Then if that's the effect on you, you can have another.' Harry stopped in the street, and, to the delight of all who had seen nothing unusual in the elegant *senhor*'s action, he kissed Clo's right hand.

'Oh, you absolute idiot!'

They both burst out laughing, then found a market, and began to bargain. They did not buy much . . . a fan, a scarf, a clockwork monkey who ran up and down a stick, some lanterns and a golden birdcage of silk canaries who sang their stuffed hearts out when you turned a key.

'It's been a wonderful day, Clo,' Harry appreciated as they climbed the stairs of the college hall of residence.

'Of course, but then it's a wonderful year, it's the Year of the Dragon. It's the magic year.'

'It only needs Ah Seng to serve up that gorgeous chicken pineapple thing for dinner and life will be complete,' Harry sighed happily.

But Amah was not serving anything, she was standing waiting at the door of Harry's flat and wringing her hands.

'All gone. All gone,' she wept.

'Chicken? The vase we borrowed? My books?'

'Second Son—Tang. All gone. Not here. He go out and not come back.'

Ah Seng dropped on her knees and began to knock her head on the floor.

CHAPTER FOUR

CLO and Harry got Ah Seng up again, then asked the customary redundant questions that concerned people do ask in times of alarm. Where had Tang gone? ... As though his mother would be wailing if she knew. Why had he gone? ... Another unproductive interrogation.

Eventually Amah calmed down sufficiently to tell them that there had been no school today, the same as there had been a stand-down at the college, and that Tang had come and asked her if he could go out for a while. He always did that, he was a good boy. Because she was making a very nice dish for supper ... Puk King Ting Arp, with duck and Hoi sin sauce ... she had said yes. That had been hours ago, now it was hours after, and Tang had not returned.

Had he carried some food? they inquired.

No, no food, for eating never worried Tang, not like First Son and Third Son.

A fishing line? Clo's heart lurched as she suggested it; it was surprising how many children here in Hong Kong could not swim, how many adults as well. The Cantonese had never embraced the pastime.

No, Amah said, no line to fish. But the question had alerted her. She recalled now that Tang had carried his butterfly net. That was more hopeful, a little boy would not go into a busy street to chase a butterfly, so at least they could rule out the crowded markets, the buzzing motorways.

But it was also mind-boggling, since, for a crammed city, Hong Kong had a surprising number of open spaces where a child could run with a net. Also lots of steep places, Clo

47

shivered, where the child, eyes only on flashing wings, could forget to watch his step and hurtle over.

However, Amah soon put Clo's mind to rest about that. Tang, it seemed, only ever 'took' a fishing line, only ever 'took' a net. He brought nothing home.

'Because he caught nothing,' Harry suggested.

No, said Amah, because he did not *try*. When he went fishing, he just sat, and when he went butterflying, he just ran. His cousin Heng had reported this. Tang, said Heng, instead of fishing became a fish, too, but only in his mind. He also became a butterfly and flew. Except, Heng had added, just now with Cousin Tang it was dragonflies instead.

... 'How far I wonder did he stray. Chasing the burnished dragonfly today?' Clo fretted. That had been a Japanese mother wondering about her little dead son running through the clouds of heaven, but here was an alive little Cantonese boy chasing earthly dragonflies ... or so they prayed.

She turned miserably to Harry.

'We've hours before dark, Clo,' he tried to cheer her. 'don't look like that. I'll rustle up as many of the staff as I can, any students I can find. There's always some around— I think they'd attend here even if it was a cyclone.'

'Typhoon,' Clo corrected dully. 'Thank you, Harry.'

Harry went out, explained the situation, then sent out his volunteers in different directions. Doctor Denning was persuaded he would be of more help staying by the telephone, Amah that she would be of better value making tea, then Clo left, too.

She went everywhere she could imagine a little boy with a butterfly net going; when no one was looking she ran to get the feeling she knew Tang would have. For she had understood perfectly when Amah had spoken of Tang not fishing but being a fish, not butterflying but being a butterfly, and she knew that his small, burnt-gold feet had per-force remained on the ground, yet nonetheless he had swum, he had soared.

She did not find Tang, she only found other searchers looking vainly, as she was looking. Desperately she came home.

The hall of residence was empty and for a joyous moment Clo thought: He's here, it's all over! Then she heard voices, listened, and knew that Father, Amah and a few others who had now returned were searching the basement.

Then spontaneously, instinctively, as if she had been waiting to do just this, as if it were inevitable, the only thing to do, Clo went, took up the phone, rang the Hotel Stella. She knew the number, she had dialled it frequently.

Ah Ming answered from Reception. Clo recognised her sweet, tinkling voice.

'Ah Ming, it's Clotilda. Is the Marques de Velira there?'

'No, not here, but do not hang up, Clotilda, I know the number and I will dial it and put you through.'

'Thank you for ever!' said Clo gratefully.

'Something wrong?' asked Ah Ming.

'I hope not.'

'I transfer you. There!'

A voice came over almost at once, a very clipped, correct voice, the voice of the Marques. He must have been in the same room.

'Yes?'

'It's I, Clo Denning.'

'Yes, Clotilda?'

But now that she had come this far, Clo wanted to go no further. What a fool she had been, a bigger fool even than at their initial meeting, as though this sophisticated man had any interest, as though he could care!

'Clotilda!' Sharply now.

'I don't know why I rang,' she faltered.

'Then I think I do. The small boy?'

'Tang ... then you've heard?'

'I haven't heard, but I know.'

'Know, *senhor*?' she echoed.

'Clotilda, why did you ring me?' he demanded.

'I—I can't say. I—I just picked up the phone. I—I just turned to you.'

'Like that?'

'Yes—I'm sorry.'

'Sorry! *Sorry!* Look, Clotilda, stay there. I will be down at once.'

'Down where?'

'At the hall of residence.'

'To help search?' she asked.

'To bring you back here.'

'Where is here?'

'Up the hill. Up the Peak. Tia's house.'

'But really yours—grace and favour,' she said absently.

'You sound hysterical. Are you hysterical?'

'No.'

'Then sit quietly and I will come. No, do not answer me, just sit. Do as I say. Obedience, Clotilda.'

'Yes,' said Clo faintly, and she did just that. She obeyed.

He was down almost at once, it was not far to come, and it was a steady descent. He came racing up the stairs and along to Harry's flat, the others still searching and calling down in the basement. This infamous flat, Clo thought, where he had slipped on the floor and she had done terrible things.

'Come, *pequena*,' he called.

'*Pequena?*' Clo looked around her, half expecting a third in the room.

'Little one,' he translated impatiently. 'But first a pen and paper.'

'Pen and paper?' she echoed.

'Or do you wish me to carve a message on the table? This will do.' He had found a pencil stump. Across the top of a newspaper he wrote in large letters:

'ALL O.K.'

'Is that right?' he asked.

'In Portuguese, you mean?'

'It would be understood in Portugal, Greece, Italy, France, what-have-you, snack bar—O.K., it is a universal expression. No, I asked if it would be all right left here?'

'If it were true.'

'Come,' was all he replied.

The big black car was waiting, a liveried chauffeur behind the wheel. He was Portuguese, and he responded quickly to Vincente's: 'Back again, Jacinto, please.'

The car shot up the very steep hill.

Clo often had come up to the Peak, just to look out and enjoy, and always she came for festivals, for there was no view in all the world as stunningly lovely as that of the Victoria Peak in Hong Kong, and no better vantage point for a display.

But she did not look out entranced now as she always did in the rattling cable tram, admiring the spectacular vista by day, the shining mosaic at their feet by night, she was too bewildered.

But no longer was she afraid; the Marques had said nothing but she knew everything was under control.

ALL O.K., he had written, so it was.

Now the car was swinging into a wide drive, and Clo had to notice. All the houses up here were palatial, but this one, she had frequently thought on her visits to the Peak, was the most wonderful of all. Among the others she always had looked at it first. One-storey ranch style, but extremely widely so, since the site needed no second elevation as it already had its own incomparable vista, it spread rather than stood behind a hedge of temple flowers, waxen cream stars completely concealing it so that it almost could not have been there at all.

The big car swung round to a side entrance ... more temple flowers, some bauhinia and azalea ... and an entire wall of windows, but all discreetly curtained, currant brocade curtains looking more elegantly Western than Oriental.

The chauffeur was opening the door, nodding acquiescence back to the Marques, who was now holding a quietening finger to his lips.

'Come, Clotilda,' the Marques whispered.

She stumbled out, even more puzzled, and when once again he put his finger to his lips, she tiptoed with him.

They went into the wide, wide house ... a little lacquer and bamboo but still predominantly Western, antique European ... then down a thickly-carpeted hall.

Here the level of the house split, and a screen had been placed across to give privacy to the room on the lower of the levels. The Senhor drew Clo behind the screen with him, a very beautiful screen in ivory, hammered to form intricate patterns, and he nodded to the space between its roses, leaves and small birds to the room beyond.

There sat an old lady in a rich black shawl over a plain black silk dress with a collaret of pearls. She wore a lace mantilla and held an ivory fan which she had opened to show the intricate designs on the fan to a small, sunflower-gold boy at her feet.

Tang.

It was a touching sight, a beautiful sight. Age and youth, and both lovely in their different ways. It should have been painted into a picture, Clo thought, or carved on a cameo brooch.

For a moment only they stood there, then Vincente quietly stepped back, taking Clo with him. They went outside again to the car, and there the Senhor dismissed

Jacinto, telling him that he himself would drive now, would drive around the Peak.

'But not far, *pequena*,' he told Clo, 'only as far away from the house that we can talk.' He reversed the big black model, went out to the street again, then accelerated up even higher to the top scenic reserve.

For a few minutes they both sat there in silence, for there was beauty here you hesitated to encroach on, the un- believable green of Fragrant Harbour far below them, over the mile-wide crossing Kowloon the raffish, looking dream- like in the distance instead of strictly commercial, people like little ants moving busily around, tiny bugs of junks and sampans. And all to the accompaniment of the trees in the small reserve sighing a sweet sad song. But—sad? Tang, the sunflower spirit, was found again.

'How did you find him?' Clo asked. 'And why did we leave him there?'

'He came up here himself,' the Senhor said, 'so there was no question of finding him, he simply ran in with his little net. He was chasing butterflies.'

'He wouldn't have caught them,' Clo assured him.

'No, I could see that. I could see he was only carrying the net so it would not look strange when he became a butterfly and flew, too.'

'You have great perception, *senhor*,' Clo blurted grate- fully. She added: 'But I'm told he is now caught up with dragonflies.'

'He is a flower of a boy,' Vincente nodded.

'A windflower? Here, then gone, as the windflowers go. We'd thought he had gone.'

'No, not gone. Not yet.'

'What do you mean?' she asked perplexedly.

'I speak idly, child.' A pause, a rather long one. 'He will not be a scholar, I think, not, anyway, an orthodox scholar. A painter or a poet, perhaps.'

'Yes.' For some reason, Clo shivered, she could not have said why.

'You are chilled, Clotilda?'

'On a day like this!'

'You shook,' he pointed out.

'It was nothing.' Yet there had been something, it had come when the Senhor had wondered what would become of Tang. A finger seemed to have touched her heart.

'*Senhorita?*' he insisted.

'When I was a child I used to say a puppydog was sitting on my grave,' she told him.

'When you shivered?'

'Yes.'

'What a child you were, and still are!'

'You did not answer my second question. Why did we leave Tang there without appearing and explaining ourselves? It seemed impolite.'

'To whom? Tia Juanita ... yes, it was Tia ... did not even know we were there. As for the will-o'-the-wisp boy ... correct?'

'Correct. So the old lady was Dona Juanita. But you said she and Isabella were not expected until tomorrow.'

'True, but women change their minds. And that is the reason we did not intrude.' The Senhor paused. 'Among others.'

'Other reasons?'

'Yes.'

'Can I know them?' she asked.

'Of course. My aunt is a stickler for etiquette, she would not have been pleased to meet you now.'

'You mean—I'm untidy?'

He looked at her with a quirk. 'Rather let us say that you are not tidy.'

'I've had a bad time,' she explained.

'My child, I am not criticising you, spare such a thought.'

'Very well, then. You were telling me about your aunt.'

'She will not, and never will, I fear, embrace more modern views than the views she holds now. To her a meeting must be formal, arranged.'

'Yet she met Tang,' Clo pointed out.

'Ah,' he said, 'and that is the final and telling reason why we could not interrupt.'

'Why, *senhor*?'

'You saw Tia.'

'Yes.'

'You saw her absorbed face.'

'Yes.'

'Then it was a moment not to be broken, it was a very precious time.'

'Can I be told?' Clo asked.

'I brought you here for that.'

He had taken out a silver case. 'I will not offer one to you,' he smiled. 'I do not think for a moment you would smoke a cheroot.'

'No, I wouldn't,' she said, 'and I've never seen you do it.'

'Not regularly, only when I wish to talk seriously.'

'Please go ahead.'

He attended to the cheroot, lit it, leaned back.

'I told you of Tia Juanita's influence on Isabella, on me, on all her nieces and nephews.'

'Aviella?'

'She is on Tia's husband's side, therefore, according to Tia's way of thinking, under a different category.'

'Not the same blood category?'

'Exactly.'

'But nieces and nephews, you said. There are more?'

'Yes, but let us not concern ourselves at the moment over that, rather to understand—and accept—that having no children of her own, Tia has all children. You will agree?'

'A little,' said Clo reluctantly, wondering at her reluctance, for it was not in her nature to be possessive.

'Both Isabella's mother, and my mother, and another sister of Tia's, died quite young, a sad family, really, but Tia remains, proud, splendid, invincible.'

'She seems indeed that,' Clo agreed.

'... Also formidable, you are thinking secretly?'

'Well—perhaps.'

'Yes, she would appear that to you, but she has a wonderful heart once you find your way to it. She was the eldest in a family of girls, and she took upon herself the responsibility of each sister. When she had no children of her own, she also took upon herself the responsibilities of the orphaned children ... myself, for I was the first, Isabella, several from the fourth daughter, also gone, as I said.'

'And the fourth daughter's children?'

'Grown-up, of course, and fortunately for them, no doubt, safely away from her sharp eyes in America. For free, relaxed America my formal aunt does *not* like, so they are undisturbed there.' He laughed. 'Free from corrective visits.'

'Yet I think you are fond of Tia Juanita,' Clo commented.

'Fond? I am devoted to her. She enrages me, she sends me hurrying to new business contacts at the other end of the world simply to get away from her, you could even say perhaps that I am a rich man solely because of the furious energy she has caused to spring in me in pure angry frustration. Yet' ... a smile ... 'I always come back.'

'But now it's widowed Isabella receiving her attention,' cheered Clo.

'Yes, although——'

'Yes, *senhor?*'

'I'll put it this way: To the Portuguese woman there is no gift like a son. The Portuguese women love their daughters, but a man child, ah!'

'I think I understand. I think you are telling me that you still will be Tia-stricken whatever happens?' Clo said kindly.

'Always. And I am saying this now to express to you *why*, most of all, we could not intrude just now. It was a moment, as I said. Tia was looking with love on a little boy.'

'I see,' said Clo.

'And you sympathise?'

'Oh, yes, I do.'

'Good, then. We will give them five minutes more, then I will go and collect the child, bring him out and take you both home.'

'Leaving me in the car while you collect him, of course.'

'Yes. I'm sorry, but what I said about Tia is true. She is of the old school, everything must be formal, arranged.'

'... Including love?' Why had she said that? Clo asked herself.

'Most assuredly love. But never worry on my account, *senhorita*. I am my own person, remember I was——'

'English-schooled.' Clo said it a little tightly. 'And as though I would worry! Please, is the five minutes up yet?'

'Clotilda, I am not understanding you.' He had put down the cheroot.

'There is nothing to understand. Can we leave, please?'

'You sound angry with me. What have I said?'

'I'm not angry,' she assured him, 'and you've said nothing.'

'Believe me, I knew what I was doing when I withdrew you as I did. It is very important to me that Tia Juanita likes you.'

'Don't you really mean *approves* of me?' Clo could not see that severe old lady liking anyone except her own kin ... and a little boy.

'Very well, approves. But, and believe me again, it would still not matter, *pequena*.'

'It certainly wouldn't matter to me.'

'I meant *me*. *Myself*. I only do what I wish, not what Tia wishes.'

'You're talking in riddles,' sighed Clo, 'and I want to go home. They'll be worried.'

'I left a note.'

'They may not have read it.'

'Then will you attend to this, *senhorita: I instructed my chauffeur Jacinto to ring down and tell them in case the note was not seen*.'

'I don't believe you.'

'Then what do you believe? Whom do you believe?'

'I—I want to go back,' she repeated.

He went as though to reply, reply quite angrily, then must have controlled himself. He started the big car and they drove down to the house.

'Where is Isabella?' Clo asked during the short journey.

'Cloistered in her room doing the embroidery things Portuguese ladies do, or no doubt my aunt believes and hopes.'

'And you? What do you believe?'

'I think Isabella is trying out a new lipstick, altering the length of a gown, mooning out of the window and wishing someone would come.'

'Someone?'

'Young, male and pleasant.'

'Not handsome?'

'Not necessarily, Isabella can supply all the good looks herself. No, that would not be a requisite.' He frowned slightly.

'Will someone come?' Clo asked.

'Undoubtedly. She is beautiful and young and ready for romance.'

'But someone suitable?'

'That is another story.' He gave his slim yet strong shoulders a slight hunch. 'But you are meaning suitable to Tia, I think, even perhaps to Isabella if she has not emerged from Tia's influence as I hoped, if she is a Condessa and not merely a Senhora.'

'But she is a Condessa,' Clo pointed out.

Again the slight shrug.

'As for me,' the Marques resumed, 'I have found the right person for her already.'

Clo considered this a moment, then hunched her own shoulders.

'Well, I'm glad it's not our worry—mine, I mean, Father's.' For some inexplicable reason she added: 'Harry's.'

Vincente turned a moment from the wheel and looked at her. 'Are you a witch? A sibyl?'

'Witches wear tall hats,' she smiled.

'Then you must be a sibyl.'

She knew what he meant, she knew he was saying she had read his thoughts, but how had Harry Ferrier been in his thoughts? Surely not in conjunction with Isabella? *Condessa* Isabella?

'You are pouting,' he accused. 'You consider the young professor your personal property?'

'No, of course not—how absurd you are! But on the subject of possession, I do consider Tang as Harry's property, not your aunt's. Kindly bring him out as soon as we reach the house, seeing I can't go and fetch him myself.'

'You are angry. I like you when you are angry.'

'Then I don't like you. At least your Tia is genuine, she is autocratic and unbending in all sincerity, not being that way but pretending she isn't.'

'Like——?' he asked coldly.

'Like you. Harry Ferrier, ordinary Australian Harry

Ferrier is the last man in the world you would really like for Isabella. Or allow.'

He let her opinion on him pass, but he insinuated:

'And you? You would not like it, either?'

'Like what?'

'What we are speaking of, *senhorita*, my cousin and the new professor.'

She shrugged. 'If it happened.'

'Of course. If it happened.'

'Then you're quite right, I wouldn't like it. Harry is too nice a person to be mixed up with any de Veliras.'

'Not de Veliras,' he corrected.

'Then connections of the de Veliras. But then, fortunately, it won't happen. They won't even meet.'

'I would not be too sure of that, *senhorita*,' he said.

'I am sure. An undistinguished ... unless you count letters ...'

'I do count letters.'

'Man from Down Under. Oh, no. There won't even be a casual encounter.'

'No, but there'll be a formal one. You'll see.'

'Then poor Harry. I'm glad it's not I.'

'You, too. Doctor Denning. All attending Tia's house.'

'We wouldn't come,' she assured him.

'I would not be sure of that, either.'

'But why would you want us?'

'Tia is a very intelligent person, she has a great regard for learning, she will love to meet Doctor Denning.'

'Also his learned successor?'

'That does raise a problem,' he agreed. 'Too young, too risky, you think?'

'Risky?' she queried.

'For a young girl like Isabella?'

'I'm young, too,' she said.

'Agreed, *pequena*, but I feel there is nothing there. If there had been it would have flowered long before this.'

'What would?'

'You and Harry.'

'Perhaps we don't rush things like the Portuguese.'

'Have *I* rushed you?'

'You're ridiculous!' Clo sighed.

'It is the Portuguese romance in me.'

'Harry will not come,' she said firmly. 'I will not come. Dad will not come.'

Again he teased: 'We'll see.'

'Will you fetch Tang, please?'

'It is done already, I told Jacinto to bring him out in five minutes.'

'Are you always obeyed?' sighed Clo.

'Always. Now I am ordering you to obey me in this.'

'In what?'

'In meeting my aunt and my cousin.'

'Formally?'

'Yes.'

'No, *senhor*,' said Clo firmly.

'Yes, *senhorita*.'

'This,' said Clo as they regained the Peak house and collected Tang, 'is goodbye, *senhor*.'

'*Bom dias.*'

'We will not be seeing you either casually or formally,' she assured him.

'If,' he inserted, 'you have your way. But I don't believe you will.' He clapped his hands for Jacinto to move forward.

When Clo went into the hall of residence everything was normal. Ah Seng was cooking the Puk King Ting Arp and had forgotten the whole affair. Harry seemed to have forgotten, too. Also her father. They were intent instead on identical white envelopes, very proper white envelopes,

with gold crests on them ... a cork tree, a ship, a *palacio*?
... and what was inside.

'Dona Juanita del Carross——' Clo began to read, then
she put the letter down.

'Oh, o!' she cried.

CHAPTER FIVE

THE maddening part about it all was her father's and Harry's eager enthusiasm. When Clo had said proudly that they would not come, and the Marques had replied that he would not be sure of that, the Senhor had been on safe ground. Doctor Denning was most definitely very pleased over the invitation, and Harry at once began wondering about clothes. It appeared that up till now he had not led a social life, and had only the grey slacks and blue shirt ... two blue shirts, he said, one for changing ... that he wore under his college gear.

'Is it suitable?' he asked Clo.

'Unsuitable ... and yet Senhor Velira told me that his aunt has a great respect for scholars, so I'm sure she'd be appeased by your gown and mortarboard if not what was underneath.'

'I'm not wearing a gown and mortar to a party!' he grinned.

'The invitation says nothing about a party, it says——'

The invitation said:

'Dona Juanita del Carross requests the pleasure of the company of Professor Harry Ferrier to dinner at the Villa Serra da Estrella on...' It gave the day, which was the day after tomorrow, then the time.

'A dinner party,' pointed out Harry.

'Dinner, no party.'

'It could grow into a party.'

'It could not. Never in a correct Portuguese household. The young Condessa Isabella will be there.'

'Good. I like a crowd of girls competing for me.' Harry eyed Clo mischievously.

'You didn't let me finish. The young Condessa, *not long widowed*, will be there.'

'Well?'

'Oh, Harry, don't be a fool!'

'At least I'm a happy fool. I'm quite anticipating a night out.'

'I am, too,' admitted Clo's father. 'I have had contact with Dona Juanita before. She wrote to me once appreciating one of my books, and asking for a more detailed explanation of several passages. I was most gratified. An author likes to know he is read with interest and intelligence. I look forward to meeting and speaking with Dona Juanita.'

'For heaven's sake, what clothes do we wear, Clo?' Harry appealed.

Clo did not know what to say. She had no doubt that the Marques would be attired very properly, very formally, even brilliantly, but she could not see this casual Australian in any of those kind of clothes, proper, formal, brilliant. She pursed her lips. 'You should wear a suit with a jacket at least,' she said.

'I have no jacket.'

'Then perhaps a navy reefer over your grey pants, one with silver buttons.'

'Gold buttons, and wouldn't I look like a sailor?'

'The best thing is for you to come across to Kowloon with me and see Lee Lan,' suggested Clo.

'Lee Lan?'

'Lee Lan does wonderful things in a short time.' Clo now was thinking of herself as well as Harry.

'Like what?'

'Clothes, you nit! Dad, you'll be perfect. Dona Juanita will approve of your grand old smoking coat with the velvet collar.'

'As old as she is,' nodded Doctor Denning. 'Yes, I'll be

right, when one has the years I have one is not expected to be a peacock. Anyway, I quite like the smoking coat myself. And you, Clo? Not denim, I hope.'

'No. No, I'm afraid, darling, you'll have to part out some dollars for me.'

'It will be a pleasure,' he assured her. 'You never dress up enough.'

'Because it doesn't appeal to me.' But it was appealing now, in fact, Clo realised, it was nagging at her. A desire to look special. Ridiculous! She would simply instruct Lee Lan to make her a new dress, nothing special at all.

'We'll go early in the morning before your first lecture,' she told Harry.

They took the Star Ferry the next day, then a rickshaw to Lee Lan's tailoring shop.

'A bit of a squeeze,' Harry said of the rickshaw, 'but I'm not complaining.'

There were many one-day tailors and dressmakers in Hong Kong, but Clo always considered Lee Lan the best. He had made her dresses when she was a child, and had always added some little touch to delight a small girl's heart ... a poised embroidered butterfly on a pocket, a bright singing bird on a bodice. Lee Lan knew Clo and liked to make for her—young women, he said, meaning it as a compliment, as lean as beanpoles were very satisfactory to put dresses on, the dresses hung as they should.

Lee Lan had agents who visited all the big liners in port to take literally hundreds of orders from both male and female passengers. All the goods were delivered on time, and they always fitted. He had a big staff, and they were always busy, but he managed personal attention now to an old customer, none other than Doctor's Daughter. Before asking Clo her needs, he went through a ritual.

How was Doctor? How was Doctor's Daughter? Was the

season pleasing Doctor? Was it pleasing Doctor's Daughter?

Father was well, she was well, the season was fine, Clo recited, and could she present Doctor's new man, Professor Ferrier.

How was Professor? Was the season pleasing Professor?

Professor, broke in Clo, wanted something to wear to a dinner—no, not exactly formal, but on the other hand not—not——

'I'm an Australian,' said Harry outrageously, 'and only used to witchetty grub tucker, but at this shindig ... this dinner...'

'I understand, Professor, and I suggest this.' This was a lightweight fabric with a safari cut jacket, casual, yet with enough inbuilt style to wear fairly formally. Harry was pleased and was whisked off to be measured. Lee Lan turned to Clo.

'A dress for yourself, Doctor's Daughter?'

'Yes.'

'I have some lovely Thai silk, newly come in. Blue shot with purple, rose shot with gold.'

'No Thai silk, Lee Lan,' refused Clo, and Lee Lan's mouth dropped open. Always his ladies loved his Thai silk. The passengers of the ships always agreed to Thai silk made in his favoured A-line.

'Also,' said Clo, 'no A-line.'

'Miss Denning!' reproved Lee Lan to show how disappointed he was in Clo. If he had not been disappointed he would have called her Doctor's Daughter.

'I've had Thai silk every time, A-line every time. Today I want—I want something different.' Clo stopped and looked apologetically at Lee Lan. He was a dear old man and he always made perfectly. To her surprise Lee Lan suddenly was all smiles.

'I understand,' he said, 'I understand that this is special, that it is to be for a very special time ... for a very special person? To think I made for you as a small duck and now I make for you as a bride.'

'No, no, Lee Lan, not a bride,' she assured him hastily.

'Then I make for you nearly a bride.'

'No, Lee Lan, you see ...' Oh, what was the use! 'Show me something, Lee Lan,' Clo directed.

The dressmaker brought out brocade, beautiful peacock bright brocade, but Clo knew it was not *her*.

Jersey, Lee Lan said, fashionable now, and lovely to drape.

Clo liked it very much, but——

'But?' asked Lee Lan, then suddenly clapped his hands. He went outside and came back with a bolt of material that he carried with reverent hands.

It was—cotton!

But cotton, Clo knew as she touched it, as she had never seen cotton before. Surely when the fluffy buds had opened in some far plantation, surely when they had gone into the plantation gin, the proud owner had never dreamed of this result: softer than silk, ethereal as a cloud, so fine, approved Lee Lan, that an entire width could pass through a ring.

'It's beautiful!' sighed Clo.

'And the colour?'

'That's beautiful, too.' It was, it was a young spring green, a green-after-rain green. 'I want it with a bodice and a gathered skirt,' Clo barely breathed.

'It will be done.'

'Today,' she added.

'Doctor's Daughter, you know my business, you know that I do only A-line for the day orders, because they are simple and more true.'

'Tomorrow, then,' she tried.

'Gathers are difficult, they take time.'

'Tomorrow, Lee Lan,' she insisted.

'Very well, then, for special occasion for special person I will send up the gown tomorrow.'

Harry came out from the men's side, everyone shook hands, and Clo and the Professor took the ferry back to Victoria.

The boxes were expected around noon the next day. Harry was in a flap in spite of Clo's reassurance that Lee Lan never let anyone down.

'But it mightn't fit when it comes,' Harry groaned.

'It will,' she assured him. 'It always does.'

'This time might be the exception.'

'Then you'll have to wear your gown and mortarboard, won't you? For heaven's sake, Professor, relax!'

Harry didn't even when the boxes with Lee Lan written across them arrived. He didn't even wait to give *tippu*, he raced inside to try the suit on, and Clo had to see to *tippu* herself.

She decided to scold him about this, and when he emerged from his bedroom she opened her mouth to do so ... then shut it again.

'Harry, you look absolutely fantastic!' He did. Lee Lan as usual had done a wonderful job.

'Yes, it's good, isn't it?' Harry pranced around. 'Do you know what, Clo? It's the first suit ... personal suit ... I've ever had.'

'Handsome, definitely handsome,' awarded Clo.

'Shucks, but I like hearing it.' Harry grinned. 'Now you do your entry.'

Clo ran out with her box and undid the string with trembling fingers; she could not remember being so excited for years.

The young spring green dress tumbled out, all swirling, unpressed pleats, all freshness and softness. Clo knew it was going to be just right even before she put it on. She pulled it over her head, gave a few wriggles, then looked at herself in the mirror. She saw she was lovely.

A few minutes before six the Senhor's big car arrived to bear them up to the Peak. Previously they had all agreed to descend then take the cable tram, for it was only a small walk from the top to the fabulous Villa Serra da Estrella. However, it was a nice start, getting into the large rich saloon, and especially welcome to Clo because it had turned windy. Her hair, too straight and too fine to hold any applied wave, would have been tousled in seconds.

As it was the car drove them right into the garages, and from there it was only several sheltered steps to the interior of the house. The Senhor stood on top of the steps, and he bowed low as they approached. A personal bow and a hand to Doctor Denning, the same to Harry, then a hand taking Clo's hand, raising Clo's hand, pressing downward a formal kiss.

'So good of you,' the Marques murmured. 'This way, please.' They moved into a hall, a different hall from the one Clo had tiptoed down before, but similarly presented. A mixture of East and West; Eastern bamboo, old Western elegance. At the end of the hall was a large reception room, and at the end of the room a raised dais, only very shallowly raised yet sufficiently to give anyone who sat on the winged chair on the dais an air of sitting on a throne. Dona Juanita del Carross looked as though she sat on a throne. She looked like royalty.

'Tia Juanita, our guests. Doctor Denning' ... evidently it was a Portuguese custom to present a senior first, or, as the Senhor turned next to Harry, were males favoured? or did it go on scholastic records? ... 'Professor Ferrier, Senhorita Denning.'

'My dear friends, Dona Juanita del Carross, my aunt.'

Dona Juanita, in black again, a collaret of some different gems, but quiet gems, nothing flashy, inclined her head graciously to Doctor Denning, a degree less graciously to Harry, but faintly antagonistically to Clo.

Why, thought Clo bewildered, doesn't she like me?

'You are very welcome,' she said. 'I have always wished to meet you, Doctor Denning, I have always read your books. Alas, I was born at a wrong time. Had I been a girl of today I would have been in your class, very eager to learn.'

'And a very good student,' nodded the Doctor. 'I could tell that from your interesting letter, which I still recall clearly. Now my own daughter Clotilda is not a student.'

'A lover of home arts, no doubt, handwork, or perhaps she paints.'

'No,' said Clo rather miserably, 'I don't do anything much.'

'So,' Dona Juanita said, and turned her attention to Harry. 'Very young, surely, to be assisting you, Doctor.'

'He's not assisting, he's taking my place.'

Dona Juanita was patently impressed with that, but she waved aside any approval.

'Young,' she said more to herself.

Any comment from Harry was prevented by the arrival of the Condessa Isabella. Clo saw her first, standing as she did a little outside the group, and she caught a sharp hurting breath. It wasn't right, it just wasn't right, for anyone to be as beautiful as this.

The Condessa had the same aristocratic features as her aunt, but on Isabella they appeared proud, not faintly hawk-like. She had blue-black hair, blue-black brows, black eyes and the creamiest skin Clo had ever seen. She was very tall and very slender, but even Lee Lan would not have described her as a beanpole. She was just—well, perfect.

One look at Harry looking at Isabella told Clo that he was thinking the same, except that he was not, not being the same sex, resenting the perfection.

'Wine,' broke in Dona Juanita a little sharply. 'Our own wine, Doctor, from our own Portuguese vineyards.'

'Not from rice,' the Doctor smiled. He got on well with the dowager, and Clo could see that Dona Juanita was favourably impressed with him.

Clo's eyes wandered to Isabella again ... and Harry, too, for the pair of them had come together almost as though they were puppets and someone had pulled strings.

They were talking very little, but they were looking a lot, brown eyes, black eyes meeting, merging. The wine had been poured, the Marques had made a toast, but the two still looked at each other over their untasted vintage.

Clo looked next to the Senhor and saw that he was looking at her, that he was crossing to her.

'Tonight I see a very wonderful thing,' he said for Clo alone. 'I see a little oak tree in its first shy leaf debut.'

'My dress?' she asked.

'With you in it.'

'Thank you. For a while I thought you were going to say something about a flower, as you did before.'

'It was you, I recall, who spoke of the little boy as a windflower.'

'I didn't mean then, I mean before then, I meant Senhorita Martinez. You called her a flower.'

'Oh, so you take heed of what I say,' he drawled.

'You said it in a public place, I couldn't *not* hear.'

'Yet you still took heed.' He seemed pleased over that. Before she could break in, Vincente said softly, for Clo's ears alone: 'I always thought of you as a little acorn, a pale gold acorn from which an oak tree might in time emerge. But you have confounded me tonight! You are already a tree. A small sweet tree in first green leaf. A shining green after rain.'

'You have a smooth tongue,' remarked Clo.

'Necessary in my business.'

'I don't think your aunt particularly likes Harry.' Clo was saying the first thing that came into her mind, she found she had to, to escape those sweet, rather disturbing words. 'Are his clothes incorrect?'

'He looks wonderful.'

'Yet he doesn't wear a formal suit like you.'

'It was not required.'

'Still, your aunt seems—well——'

'My aunt is a little wary because at one glance she can tell what could happen.' He said it rather impatiently, impatient with Clo.

'What do you mean, *senhor*?'

'Harry and my cousin, of course. Those sharp bird eyes of Tia miss nothing.'

'But——'

'Enough of that. Let us come back to ourselves.'

'Very well,' shrugged Clo. 'Your aunt definitely doesn't like me.'

'But she will,' he assured her.

'She doesn't, and she won't because——'

'Yes, *senhorita*? Because?'

'Because I won't be here to be liked.'

'You most assuredly will be here,' he said coolly. 'You may not think so, Tia may not think so, but you will be here. In the beginning as my cousin's companion——'

'What?' gasped Clo.

'My cousin's companion. You must have guessed' ... impatiently again ... 'that this was what I was talking about before. Then after that as my——'

He never finished the sentence. A maid had come in, and behind her came the elegant young woman Clo and Harry had met at the beach hotel.

'Dear Tia!' Aviella Martinez went up to the dais and kissed the old lady on both cheeks. She turned and did the same to a not very enthusiastic Isabella. Then she wheeled round on Vincente, kissed him, too, and said roguishly:

'Surprise! Surprise!'

'You have certainly surprised me,' the Senhor agreed. 'Wine, please, Lucia, and at the table another setting. Welcome, Aviella.'

The group formed one circle now, Tia still sitting like a queen, and they remained that way until dinner was announced.

The table in the adjoining room was beautifully appointed. Clo was put between her father and Harry, on the other side of Harry was Aviella, then the Marques, then Isabella ... looking now a little sulky ... then Dona Juanita.

The meal was entirely Portuguese, no touch of the East at all.

'I have been staying at the seaside,' Aviella Martinez told Dona Juanita, 'I needed the fresh air. But as soon as I heard of your arrival with Isabella, I came across, knowing you will want me.'

'Yes, I see you have come, Aviella,' Dona Juanita nodded. She looked thoughtful.

Isabella was looking sulkier than ever. Several times she went to speak, then changed her mind. The talk came round to Doctor Denning, and Dona Juanita leaned forward in interest. Everyone else remained quiet.

Eventually the dinner finished, too long and too rich was Clo's judgment, and the ladies retired to the sitting room that Clo had looked down on through a hammered ivory screen, looked down on old Dona Juanita and the sunflower boy.

Isabella at once proved herself a person of spirit. She said to Aviella: 'You remarked just now that you would be wanted. Then not by me. I can get through this period unaided, thank you.'

'Really, Isabella!' Dona Juanita reproved, but the admonition was quite mild, Clo thought.

'Someone your own age,' Aviella murmured.

'You are older than I.'

'Yet not Tia's age.'

'I do not like my age discussed, Aviella,' broke in Dona Juanita sharply, 'but I do agree that there should be someone for Isabella. Also Vincente mentioned it.'

'Did he say who it should be?' Clo heard herself actually asking it, and was shocked.

Tia Juanita was shocked, too. She gave Clo a cold look and did not answer her. Isabella on the other hand looked as though she was enjoying herself. They spoke of trivialities until the men joined them.

Now Dona Juanita sought out the Doctor again, and the two older people sat together in a corner of the room.

Harry had gravitated to Isabella once more, but Aviella never left the Senhor's side. Several times she tried to draw him away on some pretext of showing him something, asking his advice, but always the Marques eluded her.

At length he eluded her altogether. He slipped out of the room when she was not paying attention; Aviella could not have said which door he took, and she could scarcely ask. It would have been amusing to Clo had she been there to be amused. She was not. For literally she had been whisked away *with* the Senhor. One moment she was in the Baroque sitting room, the next moment in the Cantonese moonlight, but concealingly so behind a pillar.

'Success!' said the Senhor wickedly. 'Did you ever see such sleight of foot?'

'No,' admitted Clo. 'You're really awful. Now she'll come looking for us.'

'But not find us.'

'Why don't you like her?'

'Do you like everybody?' he countered.

'Most, I think.'

'Most mightn't include an Aviella. Now my most ... yes, I, too, like most people ... doesn't include her. Nor does

Isabella's most, and, I secretly suspect, Tia's. A nice person, I suppose, but——'

'I can hear steps,' Clo interrupted.

'Then quickly, into this corner!'

In spite of herself, Clo allowed him to push her into a space in the wall, built, she thought, for potted palms, but just now empty. It was a close fit.

'As close as a lickshaw,' she said aloud, 'I mean a rickshaw.'

'You utter child!' He gave a low laugh. 'How close is that?'

'Body to body instead of cheek to cheek.'

'I am a greedy person,' he said suavely. 'I would like both.'

'Really. Marques——'

'Vincente.'

'Vincente,' Clo said a little breathlessly.

She stood in silence as he was standing now in silence, and she waited, for she knew it had to come. She knew that when a man was as near to a woman as Vincente was to her that it was inevitable, predestined. She knew she had stiffened, but it was a stiffening of excitement, a rigidity of aching nerves ... but how would he know that?

He did not know. He said roughly: 'Is it that bad, then?'

'What, *senhor*?'

'What I am going to do to you, for you know I'm going to do it—is it that distasteful?'

'No ... I mean yes ... I mean ... Well, I mean—I mean, I'm inexperienced, Senhor Velira.'

'... Not any more,' he told her, and he pulled her closer, if that were possible, then deliberately began running his fingertips through her hair at the temples, then moving those long sensuous fingers over her shoulders, quite slowly and rather lightly at first, then quicker and stronger. He traced the line of her slender backbone up and down, touched the hollow of her throat, and then his head inclined forward to kiss her.

Only he did not.

He stopped suddenly, and Clo felt herself shiver with anti-climax, with disappointment ... yes, disappointment ... and she hated herself for it.

But there was no time for hate, for disappointment, for anything. The Marques was pointing down below them and saying: 'What's that?'

'It looks like a fire.'

'It is, and it would be the direction of your college hall of residence. Some festival, some crackers, would you say?'

'Perhaps. The Kitchen God Festival is on, and Amah has been doing a lot of scrubbing and scouring to please the Kitchen God. He should have a shrine outside the house, but of course the college authorities would not permit that, so Amah has put one in Harry's front room. It's his only other room apart from his bedroom, bathroom and kitchen, so he's not too happy. Also he's not happy over all the sweet food Ah Seng is cooking. You see sweet foods are said to sweeten up the Kitchen God's report on the house to head-quarters—Marques! Vincente! What are you doing?' For the Senhor was pushing her out of the aperture. He was leaping out himself.

'Raising an alarm,' he answered. 'That's no festival, no crackers, it's fire, a fire at the college. Look!'

Clo looked with him, looked at a dull red sky lit up spasmodically with brighter red lights. Yes, undoubtedly it was a fire.

'Doctor! Harry!' the Marques was calling. 'Clotilda, get on the phone at once.'

But Clo was leaving that to Aviella ... or Isabella ... or even Dona Juanita. She was shouting at them: 'Fire! Police! Ring at once!'

Then she was running out of the house and along the

street to the cable car, which was still running, for it was safely away from the college vicinity. She was boarding the tram, riding it down.

After that she was racing up to the blaze ... not nearly such a big one as it had seemed from the top, she thought vaguely.

For Clo was not looking very hard, at least not looking *and seeing*.

She simply was running blindly and calling: 'Tang! Tang! Where are you, Tang? Tang—Tang——'

She stumbled and hit her head and though it was only a small blow briefly she lost consciousness.

When she opened her eyes again she was on the settee in their own flat in the hall of residence, and the flat was in its normal order, nothing wrong at all.

Harry's flat, said the Doctor by his daughter's side, had been the only unit to be damaged. The flat was a sorry mess. He sighed.

'Tang?' asked Clo.

'Right as pie. I watched him watching the fire—I think he was being a fire god.'

'And Amah?'

'Well. Everyone's well, and everything ... except Harry's possessions and books——'

'And home. His first home.'

'Yes.'

'Poor Harry!'

'Poor college, too, they always had a scarcity of rooms.'

'What will happen to Harry?'

'He'll be put in a hotel, no doubt.'

'And Amah?'

'Amah,' said Doctor Denning grimly, 'and her welfare is not being discussed just now by the college authorities. When the firemen examined the damage, they found a burnt saucepan, a badly burnt saucepan. Sugar burns quickly, you know.'

'Of course. Sweet dishes for the God of the Kitchen so he'll give her a good report.'

'Maybe he will, but the College won't. Still' ... and the Doctor came and kissed Clo ... 'all's well. That's what really matters, darling. You're here.'

'You're here, too, Dad.'

There was a pause ... quite a long one. The Doctor was looking out of the window, probably looking at the mess and debris.

'... Yes, I'm here, too,' he said in a quiet voice. He kissed her.

Then he leaned over the settee, and, rather surprisingly to Clo, for he was not usually a demonstrative man, he kissed her again.

CHAPTER SIX

THE fire, unspectacular though it was, considerably inconvenienced the college. The hall of residence had always erred on the meagre side, and now with one unit less it simply could not cope. As the Doctor had told Clo, Harry was housed in a hotel.

It was a very good hotel, none other than the Mandarin, as Hong Kong-ish as Raffles was Singapore-ish, Clo enthused to Harry.

'Singapurian, Clotilda, and I agree it's a fine place, but it's not home.'

'Your cramped flat at the residence hall couldn't have been home, Harry.'

'Believe it or not, it was, it was my place.'

'Professor, you're nuts!' she smiled.

'No, I'm just wistful for a family background. I don't want a fine foyer, I want ... well, I want Ah Seng bringing me in the dead duck she bargained for, inviting me to pinch it to prove its freshness.'

'Then you *are* nuts. Besides, Amah is in disgrace. It has been established that she started the fire. She was making those orange slices in syrup that you dip in iced water to become toffee when the syrup caught alight. In no time your kitchen was ablaze.'

'And then my bedroom with all my clothes.'

'Yes, one pair of slacks and two blue shirts.'

'My gown and mortarboard.'

'The college will see to that,' she comforted him.

'Ah, but who will see to me?'

'You're being well seen to. The Mandarin——'

79

'Is excellent, quite fabulous, indeed, but I want—I want——'

'Yes, Harry?' Clo asked quietly, with sympathy now.

'I want to belong.'

'I see.' A pause. 'I'm sorry, Harry.'

'Sorry?'

'Sorry that I can't help you. I know you're nice and all that, but——'

'But?' He was looking at her quizzically.

'But it can't be I who helps perform that belonging.'

'You? Oh, come off it, Clo. Never you.' Harry actually laughed.

'You used to hint that you wouldn't mind it,' she reminded him.

'I did, but I'm telling not hinting now, telling you that I've changed my mind. Sorry, darling, but it's the little blue man all over again.'

'What little blue man?'

'The one in the song who bounced up one day and said to his heart's fancy: "Sorry, I don't lub you any more."'

'I don't believe you ever did—Harry——?'

'Yes, Clo?'

'Do you love—someone else?'

'It's early yet, but—yes. Yes, I do.'

'Someone I know?'

'Yes.'

'Not——'

'Yes.'

'Oh, Harry,' she sighed, 'you utter fool, you can't fall in love with nobility.'

'Portuguese nobility?'

'Any. I'm not being derogatory, just telling you that it wouldn't work. She's a countess.'

'So?'

She added, 'She's recently widowed.'

'Not that recently. I asked her.'

'You asked her!'

'What do you think I was talking about all the time I was with her, Applied Pacific Sciences?'

'Father was talking about them with Dona Juanita.'

'This is the Condessa and me.'

'Oh, no, Harry, it mustn't be,' she said ungently. 'Forget it at once. Anyhow, how did the Condessa come into this Mandarin Hotel thing?'

'She walked in.'

'I meant into the subject of the Mandarin ... Harry! *Harry!* you're not telling me that Isabella actually went there?' They were now sitting on a bench in the college grounds, and Clo was looking disbelievingly at Harry.

'She did,' he assured her.

'She shouldn't have and you shouldn't have.'

'I agree. It made it all the worse when she went again. A fine foyer, Clo, never makes a home.'

'Neither would that Villa Serra da Estrella on the hill.'

'Like to bet on it?' Harry grinned.

'Dona Juanita would never accept you.'

'Yes, she does pose a problem,' Harry agreed.

By common, unspoken consent they had left the vexing problem at that point and come to Amah.

'Has Ah Seng been dismissed in disgrace?' Harry asked.

'Oh, no, just reprimanded. But the worry is that there's no room for her and Second Son Tang. We have them now, but heaven only knows how they fit in. Amah will have to go to the country to a relation, I expect.' Clo bit her lip, for that would mean taking with her the sunflower spirit.

'Bad show,' sympathised Harry, then he glanced at his watch, yelped and crossed to his waiting class.

Certainly, thought Clo again later, their unit was not as comfortable as it used to be. The Doctor grumbled mildly in the days that followed, and Clo tried to get used to someone always about the place, either leaving in a hurry from a forbidden room when you entered unexpectedly, or hanging around the stairs. Also, the household bills were higher, as there were more mouths to feed. Poor Amah had declared that since it had been established as her fault she would eat nothing, or very little, but she soon forgot that. Tang, of course, never ate anything, or you never saw him eating, so he was not counted, but it did fret Clo that the little boy, who at least had had a small boxroom to himself, now had to share their own boxroom with three others.

The Marques came down one day. It was over a week since the fire, and Clo greeted him coldly. It had been a worrying time, and he could have come before this. Anyway, prior to the moment of the fire's discovery there had been another moment, a moment surely that had called for something more than ten days' absence.

'Ten days, *senhorita*? You counted them?' the Marques took Clo up immediately.

'No, of course not, I just picked on ten and merely remarked that it had been ten days since we saw you.'

'You counted,' he repeated.

'Harry is at the Mandarin,' said Clo abruptly. 'He doesn't care for it.'

The Marques evinced no surprise.

'He says it's not family,' Clo went on. 'He wants family.'

Again no surprise.

'He says a fine foyer doesn't make for happiness, he would even prefer his flat, meagre though it was.'

'. . . And his proximity to you?'

'Oh, no, that's over. It never began, but it's still over.'

'So,' said the Marques, and he tapped the tips of his long fingers together, a habit of his when he was thinking.

A few moments went by in silence. Clo broke them sulkily.

'I told Harry he was well off.'

'When he wasn't?'

'What, *senhor*?'

'There is nothing like home, Clotilda, be it a villa or a *castelo*.'

'Or a *palacio* with a cork tree beside it and a ship in the distance.'

'Did anyone ever tell you that you were a particularly detestable child?'

'Yes—you.'

He bowed.

When he spoke again, it was about Harry.

'I can sympathise with him, I have all along, but knowing it would only be temporary I did not break into the American journey I had to make.'

'You have been to America?'

'Yes, on urgent business, otherwise I would have been here before.'

'You were not needed,' she shrugged.

'No, *senhorita*?'

'No.' Clo paused. 'You just said temporary for Harry. It's going to be a very long temporary—the College Board don't anticipate a repaired and renewed unit for months.'

'Quite true, it would take that long, but my old friend, of course, will not be left in the Mandarin Hotel until such time as the unit is ready.'

'Where, then? Some other hotel?'

'No, with me, naturally I assumed you would know that.'

'I didn't know it,' she told him, 'nor did Harry.'

'He knows it now. I called on him before I called on you. I left him packing his bags.' There was a slightly ironical smile as he informed her that Harry had been dealt with first.

'Oh,' said Clo, not able to think of anything else.

The Marques when he spoke again had changed from Harry to Amah.

'Where is Ah Seng?' he asked.

'Here with us.'

'And the child?'

'Here.'

'Where do you put them all?'

'In the boxroom, in the corridors, in the laundry, on mats outside doors ... you must have stumbled over someone as you came in.'

'Well, I did see several.'

'Several hundred,' said Clo crossly; she felt cross, this man was irritating her.

'Seeing they get on your nerves——' he began.

'I never said so.'

'All the same, you'll be pleased to hear that Harry's ex-household staff will move up the hill with Harry.'

Clo wheeled round at that. 'You mean Amah will be going up to the Villa Serra da Estrella, too?'

'Yes, and taking the child.'

'Amah won't be happy,' said Clo.

'Before I left for America I had a private word with her and I think she will,' he told her.

'She won't, she'll be the only Cantonese staff.'

'Yes, the rest are Portuguese, but that will make her exclusive, and she'll enjoy that. In a very short time, I do believe, *deem-sums* or their equivalent will be creeping into our menu. A good thing, I think; I often consider we eat a little stuffily.'

'You—you said Tang will go, too.'

'Naturally.'

'Then no,' she said firmly.

'What, *senhorita*?'

'No, no, *no*. I will not let Tang leave!'

His brows had risen steeply, they almost seemed to reach the lower peak of his hair. 'Are you in a position to refuse?' he demanded coldly.

'I still say no.'

'Then there is only one answer, isn't there?'

'What, Marques?'

'You must come, too.'

'You're being ridiculous!' she snapped.

'I am being serious, indeed I have never been more serious in my life.'

'How could I go up there?' she demanded.

'The same as Harry is going, just pack your bag and proceed.'

'My place is here with Father.'

'There would also be a wide-open door for the Doctor. Tia thinks most highly of him.'

'You didn't hear me out,' she protested. 'My place is here, taking and fetching for the staff, posting their letters, buying their personal things.'

'You are officially employed?'

'No, but——'

'You are paid?'

'Certainly not, but——'

'Then you are unnecessary, you are expendable.'

'I've never wanted pay, Dad sees to that. I've simply been glad to be of help, to fill in my time.'

'Oh, your time will be filled in,' the Senhor promised, 'as companion to Isabella I should think you would not have a spare moment.'

'The answer is in the negative, a very strong negative. Anyway, Tia ... Dona Juanita would never accept me. I doubt if she will ever accept Harry.'

'You are forgetting one thing,' he interrupted.

'Oh, yes, I recall now, grace and favour.'

'Exactly. Also, *senhorita*——'

'Yes, *senhor*?'

'In Portugal what a man says is law.'

'Even to a lady of Tia's venerable age?'

'Yes,' he shrugged carelessly, 'the man is always obeyed.'

'You are,' said Clo deliberately, 'the original male chauvinist pig.'

'Thank you, *senhorita*. I will go now, leaving you something to think over.'

He went.

And Clo thought.

She did not think long. She had a second guest.

Ah Seng's sister-in-law, now the Dennings' Amah, came in with Dona Juanita del Carross, and her eyes were slits of excitement ... but Dona Juanita's eyes were veiled.

She was in black, as always, the first pearl collaret again, but the mantilla she wore over her hair was not a lace one but a discreet, concealing daytime silk.

Amah, without being told to, brought out a chair; she seemed very much in awe of the aloof visitor.

Dona Juanita shook hands with Clo and said, 'No, no tea,' so Clo told Amah no tea.

When the amah had gone, Dona Juanita inquired as to the Doctor's health, Clo's health, the weather, the likelihood of typhoons this year.

'It's the Year of the Dragon,' Clo heard herself murmur.

'Yes. That is so—*Senhorita*, I came about Professor Ferrier.'

'Yes, Dona Juanita?'

'I do not consider it a good thing for him to come up to the Villa Serra da Estrella.'

Clo privately agreed with her, but, perversely, she found herself disagreeing.

'He is homeless,' she pointed out, 'if you go along the corridor you can see what the fire did to his digs.'

'His?'

'Apartment,' Clo explained. 'It's burned out.'

'Very unfortunate, but he is comfortable now in the Mandarin?'

'Comfortable, but not happy.'

'Why?' demanded the old lady.

'He was an orphan. To him the apartment became home. He doesn't care about luxury, he wants a home.'

'That's what I am afraid of,' Dona Juanita said. She bit her lip, probably angry with herself that she had said this to the girl. Then she straightened her shoulders, if such were possible in an already ramrod figure, and said:

'*Senhorita*, there is something I must say.'

'Say it, Dona Juanita.'

'My niece is inexperienced.'

'She is a widow, Dona Juanita.'

'But she is still inexperienced in the ways of the world ... of the *young* men of the world.'

'Yet she was English-schooled.' Now Clo was saying it.

'She had a strict Portuguese upbringing—I should know, I reared her myself. To your eyes, no doubt, I did it wrongly—too much care, too much precision, too much attention to rules.'

'Her years in England would have cancelled that, I think.'

'I can see the new, untrammelled point of view, *senhorita*, but I cannot accept it.'

'Not you, perhaps, Dona Juanita, but Isabella?'

'Oh, Isabella will accept it, I have no two thoughts on that; already she has told me she will not wait the prescribed years of widowhood.'

'She is young,' said Clo placatingly.

'That is so, and he, the Conde, undeniably was old. Still in my time such a thing would not have been done. It is different today, so I must concede ... *but concede only to someone suitable for Isabella*. You understand?'

'No.'

'This young man whom my nephew proposes to bring into the house——'

'Professor Ferrier.'

'—Is unsuitable. I have nothing specific against him, but it can't be, not now, not ever.'

'But bringing him into the house doesn't mean he will propose marriage and Isabella will accept him.'

'You think not? I think otherwise. I saw the looks that passed between them that first night of their meeting.'

'Dona Juanita,' ventured Clo, 'had you been young, under similar circumstances, and met say—my father, would you have spoken like this?'

'The Doctor? The Doctor is a wonderful man, a man of wonderful learning.'

'My father says that Harry will be more than that one day.'

Dona Juanita began touching a rosary at her waist.

'You make it hard for me,' she reproached, 'when you include your father.'

'I'm sorry,' said Clo, 'but it's the truth.'

'Perhaps so, perhaps not, that is my answer to your unfortunate question. If I had been young and alone like Isabella, who knows? But I do know that my parents would have objected, and that that is why I must object now. A nobody. Even an orphan, you said.'

'Yes, I said that,' Clo answered sadly, sad that anyone could be so hard.

Dona Juanita swallowed. For a few moments she said nothing, then she started on another angle.

'You yourself, *senhorita*.'

'Yes?'

'What do you feel about this young man?'

'Harry Ferrier? He's the greatest. I'm terribly fond of him, I—— Oh, Dona Juanita!' For Dona Juanita del Carross was smiling triumphantly, getting to her feet, preparing herself to leave.

'Then surely,' the old lady said, 'you would not like him in a house with such a girl as Isabella? Oh, you are very pretty, child, don't look forlorn like that, but Isabella is

Isabella, *Condessa* Isabella. She has years of proud stock behind her, riches, aristocracy, and she has a regal beauty a mere if attractive little girl like you never could emulate. How could you hope to keep your young man?'

'He is not my young man,' Clo insisted.

'And never would be once he came to the villa. *Senhorita*, I'm sorry I have had to say this ... sorry for something else I must say.'

'Keep saying, Dona Juanita, nothing can hurt me much more than I am hurt now.'

'Very well then.' A pause. 'My nephew Vincente.'

'The Marques.'

'Yes. I think he is amused by you.'

'Amused?' questioned Clo.

'That is the word, I believe. He has never met anyone quite like you before, and it piques him. But, the same as it is with Professor Ferrier, it cannot go any further than that.'

'You don't rule him, Dona Juanita, he has told me on several occasions that no one tells him what to do.'

'True, that is the Marques in him. But when it comes to it, *senhorita*, he would know his true path, and that path would not have you standing in it. Do you understand?'

'Yes,' snapped Clo, 'I understand that you are a tiresome, arrogant, meddling old woman. Please go!'

They were strong words, but Dona Juanita was equally strong.

'I am sorry I had to speak as I did,' she said, 'but it has been for the best. I think we comprehend each other now. You and Mr Ferrier will remain the good friends of our family, but you will forget any thoughts you might have had, and the young Professor will not take up residence in the villa.'

'I think his things have already gone from the Mandarin,' said Clo.

'They will be returned.'

'Along with Ah Seng?' Clo asked. 'I was given to believe that Harry's housekeeper would be transferred to the villa with Harry.'

'That was the arrangement.'

'Then she will be returned?' A pause. 'Also Tang?'

There was a sharp silence in the room, it was almost as though a whistle had shrilled at the end of a shift. Then the next shift started. Action started. Dona Juanita fairly whirled round on Clo.

'Tang?' she demanded.

'I said Tang.'

'He remains with me, of course.'

'Of course he doesn't, he is the child of Harry's servant and stays with Harry.'

'The Professor cannot house him and his mother in a hotel, they have not been there at any time, they have been here, and now, even though the Professor does not come, they will follow the original plans and come to me.'

'Oh, no,' contradicted Clo, 'they will stop where they are.'

'In this flat?'

'Yes, Dona Juanita.'

'They must be overcrowded,' the old lady observed haughtily.

'Lamentably so, Tang is sharing a small boxroom with several others.'

'It cannot be!' Dona Juanita wrung her hands.

'It will be, though, we have more right to Tang, whereas you have no right at all.'

'I love him.'

'I love him, too,' Clo pointed out.

'You are a very stubborn person, Miss Denning.'

'Australians can be as stubborn as Portuguese,' Clo assured her.

'I have come to care for the little boy. My niece and

nephew do not know this, but I will tell you: although I am childless now I did have a child once—a boy child. He died at a very early age.'

'I'm sorry,' said Clo sincerely.

'If you were you'd let Tang go.'

'*I* might *never* marry, Dona Juanita, I might never have a son, even one who dies at a very early age, so while I can I'll have Tang.'

'You make a hard bargain.'

'Bargain?'

'The Professor.'

Clo looked out of the window and said: 'Your chauffeur has returned.'

'I will leave.' That was all Dona Juanita replied.

Clo watched her go out of the door, down the stairs.

Half an hour later the telephone shrilled. Clo beat Amah to it and picked up the receiver.

'Clotilda?' It was the Marques.

'Yes.'

'I said you were a witch, didn't I?'

'Witches wear tall hats,' she said.

'Very well, a sibyl, then.'

'Sibyls foretell.'

'Well, something to do with magic.'

'Abracadabra!' she laughed.

'Clotilda, be serious. I have something to announce.'

'Announce it,' she invited.

'You did it!' he told her.

'What, *senhor*?'

'Changed Tia's mind about Harry, you woman of magic. I'll never know how, not with an opponent like Tia, but you did.'

'Yet you really knew all along,' Clo reminded him. 'You knew you just had to issue an order. Your house, *senhor*, strictly grace and favour, you held the whip hand.'

'True, and I was determined, but I wanted this thing amicable, I wanted Tia coming and saying, if a little frozenly: "He can come." '

'Which she did?'

'Yes.'

'And he is coming?'

'Of course—You don't sound as elated as I thought, could it be you're *not* so happy over this closer settlement?'

'Closer settlement?'

'Of Harry and Isabella.'

'It could be, but it's not.'

'Words,' he said angrily. 'Idle words. So you're still that way with Harry?'

'I never was. Did anyone ever tell you that slang from a Portuguese Marques sounds abhorrent?'

'No, but you are telling me now. Clotilda——'

But Clo had put down the phone.

She went out to tell the Doctor all that had happened ... well, nearly all. All, anyway, to do with Harry. Her father had become very fond of Harry, he had been grieved about what had occurred. He would be pleased now that his young successor was to be taken into the bosom of a family. Clo's lip curled at the way she had described it. A very hard, cold bosom, she thought.

But the way she would tell it to Dad would be very different ... and she wouldn't mention the other topic, the topic of Vincente Velira and herself, at all.

She went out to the kitchen and asked Amah if she had seen the Doctor.

'No. No see Doctor. Want to see Doctor, too, to show him velly lovely pork for dinner.'

'So you haven't seen him?'

'No, missie.'

Clo next went out to their little verandah, their lesser look-out than the Peak and the Villa Serra da Estrella, and peered around. The nearer enigma of Hong Kong presented itself to her, the ever-present street markets intruding almost up to the elegant harbour-front with its plying trams, its fashionable people compared to its picturesque people only some hundred yards away in the backdrop.

Yes, hundreds of people, Clo thought, but she couldn't see Dad.

She went to the college library ... it was stand-down day, so there were no lectures ... she inquired at several of the other dons' units.

No Doctor Denning.

She walked to a corner park, a favourite considering place of his. She went to a little store where he often had a word with the storekeeper.

No Doctor Denning.

Now it was becoming a little like Tang, except that Tang was a small boy, and he had carried a butterfly net. Father was adult, responsible, but he was still ... and two hours later Clo faced up to this ... nowhere to be found.

This time she did not take up the phone and reach out instinctively to the Marques, she rang the Mandarin. By sheer luck Harry had returned from his new lodgings to pick up something he had left behind. He came to the phone at once.

'Gone? But where?' Again the idiot concerned questions.

'I don't know, I just don't know, Harry,' she sighed.

'Stay where you are. Don't go looking or we'll have you to find as well—Clo, are you attending?'

'Yes, I am attending, but Harry——'

'Yes, girl?'

'... I'm afraid.'

'You're a goose. He's crossed the harbour to some bookshop where he's heard he can pick up a certain volume he can't get here. Yes, that will be it. Don't move, honey.' Harry put the phone down.

Clo didn't move. She sat obediently beside the receiver waiting. She drank the tea Amah brought, still waiting.

But there was no panic now, no urgency, for there was nothing to know; as far as Clo was concerned, she knew it already. She remembered that extra ... goodbye? ... kiss, and she knew that Dad had left her. People do know sometimes when it is someone they love.

Doctor Denning was found on the Star Ferry. The boat boy described how he had become alerted when the old gentleman had not got out at either end, not at Kowloon, nor at Victoria Hong Kong side. When this had happened for several trips, the boy had gone over, and seen ... tears now, for the Cantonese always had tears ready ... that the dear old man had died.

'He loved the ferry,' Clo said quietly. 'We used to go over just for the ride, my mother, my father, me. We loved to look out at all there was to see.' Ships, Clo remembered, fishing boats, people plying them, shoreside grottoes and pavilions, gardens, skyscrapers, wharves, teeming markets.

Dad had loved it all, and now he had died beside it. The old scholar had gone to the mother Clo barely remembered with the latest account of it.

'It was a good way to go,' Harry said softly.

'But it's not good,' said Clo brokenly, 'to be left behind.'

CHAPTER SEVEN

EVERYONE circled around Clo in the days that followed, bringing their tears, their comfort, in the case of Lee Lan the dressmaker a white dress, since white to the Cantonese was the colour of mourning, and since Lee Lan knew Clo's measurements and knew, too, that although he had made up many colours for her, he had never made white.

Cards came from the Chinese University, phone messages from prominent figures, cables, letters and personal visits from friends.

Dona Juanita sent flowers, but not to the chapel but to Clo, and Clo appreciated her choice, for she had ordered the national windflower, or anemone as Westerners know it, instead of the formal blossoms Clo would have expected of her.

Clo liked the message, too: 'The light shineth in darkness.' She had inherited from the Doctor an appreciation of biblical literature, and smiled wanly at once: 'St John.'

When the Marques came down she asked him to thank Tia Juanita.

'Yes, she shows a good heart at times.' A sigh. 'Infrequent times.'

'What do you mean, *senhor*?'

'We are having little what-do-you-call them?' he explained.

'Spats?'

'Yes. Indifferences.'

'Yet you have so much in common,' she remembered.

'I could argue that with you ad infinitum, but just now I have not the time.'

95

'You are off again?' she queried.

'To England, *senhorita*.'

'But not on this occasion,' Clo smiled bleakly but still a smile, 'to be schooled.'

'Ah, you are getting better.'

'A little. The pain is still great.'

'All amputations are. Do you feel better enough to talk?'

'Talk about what?' she asked.

'You. What you are going to do?'

'Going to do?' Clo looked at him bewildered, even stupidly. 'What do you mean?'

'You can't stay here, you are not a member of the staff.'

'No, but I've always been here. For twenty years I've been here.'

'That still does not assure your residence here, Clotilda.'

'I suppose not. I suppose I'll have to think of something somehow, some time.'

'What?'

'I don't know. I just don't know.'

'Then do not worry until the necessity arises.'

'Necessity?' she queried.

'Oh, Clo, Clo—— Look, I am leaving now. I have no doubt you will still be here when I come back. Then we can really face up to it. Face up together?'

'Face up to what?'

'You, and where you are to—— Oh, never mind. *Bom dias, pequena*.'

'Goodbye.'

'I did not say that, I did not say *adeus*, I said *bom dias*.'

'Isn't it the same?'

'It is only a temporary wish, said when one will be back soon. Say it after me. *Bom dias*.'

'*Bom dias*,' Clo said obediently.

He crossed to her, considered her a moment, then stooped down and lightly kissed her, a feather of a kiss,

These three exciting Harlequin romance novels are yours FREE!

Lucy Gillen sets this romance among the wild lochs and mountains of Scotland. **"A Wife for Andrew"** is a touching account of a young governess, her dour yet compassionate employer and the children in his care who suffer at the hands of a jealous woman.

In Betty Neels' **"Fate Is Remarkable"** Sarah's "marriage of convenience" is dramatically altered. Just as Sarah was getting ready to tell Hugo that she'd fallen in love with him, a lovely woman from Hugo's past shows up…

In **"Bitter Masquerade"** by Margery Hilton, mistaken identity is the basis of Virginia Dalmont's marriage. When Brent mistook her for her twin sister Anna, she wondered if her love was strong enough to make up for the deceit…

I n the pages of your FREE GIFT Romance Treasury Novels you'll get to know warm, true-to-life people, and you'll discover the special kind of miracle that love can be. The stories will sweep you to distant lands where intrigue, adventure and the destiny of many lives will thrill you. All three full-length novels are exquisitely bound together in a single hardcover volume that's your FREE GIFT, to introduce you to Harlequin Romance Treasury!

The most beautiful books you've ever seen!

Cover and spine of all volumes feature distinctive gilt designs. And an elegant bound-in ribbon bookmark adds a lovely feminine touch. No detail has been overlooked to make Romance Treasury books as beautiful and lasting as the stories they contain. What a delightful way to enjoy the very best and most popular Harlequin Romances again and again!

A whole world of romantic adventures!

If you are delighted with your FREE GIFT volume, you may, if you wish, receive a new Harlequin Romance Treasury volume as published every five weeks or so—delivered right to your door! The beautiful FREE GIFT VOLUME is yours to keep with no obligation to buy anything.

Fill out the coupon today to get your FREE GIFT VOLUME.

Three exciting, full-length Romance novels, in one beautiful book!

FREE GIFT!

Dear Ellen Windsor:

Yes, please send my FREE GIFT VOLUME with no obligation to buy anything. If you do not hear from me after receiving my free gift volume, please mail me the second volume of Romance Treasury. If I decide to keep the second volume, I will pay only $4.97 plus a small charge for shipping and handling. I will then be entitled to examine other volumes at the rate of one volume (3 novels) every five weeks or so, as they are published. Each volume is at the low price of $4.97 plus shipping and handling and comes to me on a 10-day free approval basis. There is no minimum number of books I must buy. I can stop receiving books at any time simply by notifying you. The FREE GIFT VOLUME is mine to keep forever, no matter what I decide later.

Please print clearly

C78 – 5R

_____
Name

_____
Address

_____
City   State   Zip

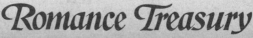

Romance Treasury

Offer expires December 31, 1978.

Detach and Mail
Post Paid Card
TODAY!

gentle, considerate, kind. Quite sexless.

Still only half aware of things, Clo began to pack. She made neat piles of all her father's books, then sought out the college Director as to what to do with them.

He sat her down in the chair opposite to him and began to fiddle with a letter opener.

'The books ... oh, yes, *they* will be easy.'

'Meaning, Director?'

'Meaning, dear, that *you* are the difficult one.'

'In what way?' she questioned.

'I hate saying it coldbloodedly like this, but I can't think of any other way, and you don't seem to have thought of it yourself.'

'Thought of what?'

'That you can't stay on here.'

'That I—oh, I see. No, of course I can't, can I? The Marques mentioned it, and I entirely agree.'

'Do you, Clo? Has it come to you then that your home unit is strictly a family unit and essentially for the next family intake? Has it come to you that you have no right, apart from the permission springing from our respect of your father and our love of you, to be here now?'

'It hadn't,' she confessed. 'Now it has.'

'We would love to keep you as you are, doing our personal errands, attending to our private wants. But the college, as you know, is individually endowed, and there's no money left over as could be expected in a large government academy of learning.'

'Oh, I know, Director,' Clo nodded.

'Good, then.' The Director heaved a sigh of relief. 'You won't be hassled, of course. Any ideas?'

'Ideas?' she echoed.

'As to what to do? Where to go?'

'Oh—oh, no, not at present, but no doubt it will come.'

'No doubt at all. And how we'll miss our little messenger

girl!' The Director leaned across and patted Clo's hand in a fatherly fashion.

'You must see the bank manager,' he said next.

'The bank manager? Oh, to know how things are.'

'Exactly, dear.'

'I'll do that, Mr Fothergill,' she assured him.

'There will be, of course,' Mr Fothergill said wretchedly, 'no—er—pension for you.'

'No what, Mr Fothergill?'

'No sum of money like there would have been for a staff employee. You were never officially engaged here, Clo.'

'No,' she said flatly.

'Also' . . . more wretchedly still . . . 'nothing to offer you, not in a privately endowed college, a college whose benefactors don't even live here in Hong Kong, and to whom any requests have to be written, not made personally.'

'Please, Mr Fothergill, I understand.'

'There's only one more thing.' Now Mr Fothergill was even more remorseful.

'Tell me,' said Clo, resigned.

'Your flat is needed—well—moderately soon.'

Clo gulped. She did not like the sound of that 'moderately'. Was this her final notice? She tightened her already tight hands.

'How "moderately", Director?'

'At once.'

'I see,' Clo said.

Presently she asked: 'And our . . . *my* . . . present Amah and her family? She was recently widowed, you know.'

Mr Fothergill held up a soothing hand. 'Don't distress yourself, my dear,' he said, glad to have something constructive to say at least, 'the next family will need a servant, and your Amah and her children will continue on. You will' . . . before Clo could pose any more questions . . . 'see the bank manager?'

'Yes. This afternoon.'

After lunch Clo put on a fresh blouse, combed her acorn hair and descended to the bank with which they had dealt. 'They' was rather a wrong word, Clo grimaced, she had only ever had a savings account, and as fast as she put anything in she had drawn it out again. But then there had never been much to deposit, only the pin money that Dad had been able to spare. She had never known what the Doctor earned, neither father nor daughter had had the slightest interest in money, but she had guessed, being a private concern, it would not have been a very large amount, especially with their two-bedroomed unit deducted, plus their housekeeper, plus several other necessary expenses. Also, although Dad's books had been hailed as quite remarkable in their field, by no stretch of the imagination could they ever be termed popular or bestsellers. Just as well, Clo thought, our likes had been simple likes, otherwise we would have been in trouble.

Within five minutes in the bank, for she was ushered into the manager's office at once, Clo found that even with a simple taste she already was in trouble. There was no money, no money at all.

'But——' she faltered.

'Really,' the manager fretted, 'the college should have told you all this, not left it to me.'

'Told me what?'

'Told you about the Doctor.'

'About my father. Yes?'

'For years, ever since his sixtieth birthday, the good doctor had been attached to the college only out of grace and favour.'

'Oh, yes, grace and favour.'

'The authorities still thought as much of him, and he performed his work as wonderfully, but they had a previous strict law regarding age.'

'Yet Dad was allowed to stay on?'

'At,' said the manager, as wretched as the Director had been, 'at a greatly reduced salary.'

'Dad never said!' Clo sighed.

'Didn't want to worry you, no doubt, although, being Doctor Denning, probably after the initial reduced pay cheque he never even noticed.'

'No, he wouldn't have noticed,' Clo said warmly.

'You can well imagine, Miss Denning, what a ruin your double unit and what goes with it made of that reduced cheque.'

'Yes, I can.'

The manager sighed, 'If only your father had trained you for something!'

'I had no brains,' Clo said.

'Not necessarily for the college, but for—well, clerical work, typing, perhaps kindergarten teaching.'

'I wouldn't have minded that.' Clo was thinking of a whole class of sunflower Tangs.

'Fashion co-ordinator,' went on the manager, but his voice faltering a little as his eyes fell on Clo's denim skirt and white blouse.

'Anything,' he finished, 'just anything would have helped. But he kept you at home. Why?'

Clo said vaguely, feeling vague, feeling unreal:

'To cook lamb.'

'What, my dear?'

'He didn't like the way Amah cooked lamb. Mr Smith, please come out with it.'

'Money?' Mr Smith said directly.

'Yes.'

'I told you, Miss Denning, practically nothing. Oh, a few Hong Kong dollars once the last pay comes in and the unit is deducted and we add the very small amount left in the savings section, but——'

'Nothing to speak of?'

'Nothing at all to speak of. I'm sorry. We all of us loved Doctor Denning.'

'I know,' said Clo, 'I know. Don't worry, I'll get by.'

'Perhaps some Hong Kong family will need a governess, that is' ... hastily ... 'a nursery or elementary governess. Or perhaps you could go to your relatives in Sydney ... or was it Melbourne?'

'Yes,' said Clo, leaving him to work it out for himself, for she had no relations in either place, to her knowledge she had no relations anywhere. Her mother had been an 'only', her father an 'only', and they had left Australia twenty years ago.

'Then you can go to them,' the manager said thankfully. 'If you wait outside, dear, I'll have a cheque drawn up. It's not quite as the law likes things to be done, but I'm sure in this case and with such a small amount involved ...'

Clo went outside and sat down. When the balance was drawn up, and the cheque given to her, she walked round the harbourside for a while, passing the big business palaces of Victoria Hong Kong side, Statue Square, the young people in their latest fashion clothes, the old people in their traditional Cantonese, the large trading houses, the glitter hotels.

But it was to a little side street café where she had often gone with Father that she turned finally. She took a window seat in small, curtained Tea and Cake.

There she looked at the cheque again, at the deleted passbook.

Account Closed. Softly, unobtrusively, Clo began to weep.

Because they were Cantonese, no one in Tea and Cake commented when Clo paid the bill and went out again with the flowered pot of jasmine brew untouched. They just watched with sad eyes, sad for Clo, and they bowed.

Clo walked up the hill, slowly because it was a very steep gradient, slowly because there seemed no life left in her, then went into the hall of residence, past Harry's ruined room which was now being repaired by an army of little deep gold men who worked like bees and never stopped for elevenses and never looked up. She felt she wanted to be like them and look down, too, look for ever. But in a few moments she had to look up, look up at Isabella, for she was taller than Clo. What was Isabella doing here?

Isabella, dressed in silver grey to concede to bereavement procedure but also, no doubt, because it did stunning things to her already stunning looks, came at once to Clo and threw her arms round her—no Portuguese formality here.

'You poor sweet! I have been thinking about you even without Harry.'

'You mean without Harry telling you to.'

'Yes, and Vincente.'

'Vincente?' Clo queried.

'He is very concerned about you. He has even ordered Tia Juanita.'

'Ordered what?' Clo searched the girl's face. 'Ordered what, Isabella?' ... the first name came naturally after all they were contemporaries.

'Ordered Tia to accept you.'

'The Marques did?'

'Yes. He said you must come as well as Harry. Clo, I can't go on as I am, with no one to talk to.'

'In that big house filled with people!'

'No one my own age,' Isabella amended.

'What about Harry?'

'Harry' ... a pout ... 'is not in the house, he is in an annexe.'

'But handy?'

'Oh, yes' ... a dimple this time ... 'very handy.'

'What did the Marques say to your aunt? No doubt he

used my father's death to try to persuade her.'

'Vincente never tries, he does, and he also never persuades, he achieves. Another thing, Clo, he said what he did before Doctor Denning's death. Oh, he said it later, too, but it was not just announced to Tia in a mood of pity.'

'He said——?'

'Isabella must have younger company. You will ask Clotilda Denning.'

'And Tia Juanita?'

'She said no, no and no.' Isabella giggled. 'But she still knew it was inevitable.'

'That she ask me?'

'That you come. Vincente always gets what he wants.'

'But I'm not coming,' said Clo firmly.

'Oh, Clo, please!'

'No.'

'Why? Don't you like me?'

'I hardly know you, but I do like you.'

'Then?' persisted Isabella.

'Your aunt doesn't like me.'

'Aunt likes no one, not, anyway, on the surface, but she'll come round,' Isabella assured her.

'I won't be there when she does.'

'Clo——'

'Listen, Isabella, I'm as desperate as a girl could be, but not that desperate.'

'How desperate?'

'To live in a house with a woman who disliked me.'

'And one who likes you,' reminded Isabella. 'I.'

'It would be unthinkable!' Clo insisted.

'Unthinkable not to come. Yes, you must do it. You see I know how you stand.'

'Stand?'

'For accommodation.'

'How would you know that? Oh—Harry.' Undoubtedly

it would be Harry, he would be aware of college requirements, he would know about her marching orders.

'Yes, Harry. So you have no choice, have you?'

'But *you* have, Isabella, you could have any girl in Hong Kong. A Portuguese girl, your own age. Or you could have that cousin Aviella.'

'*Not* a cousin, a niece of Tia through her late husband. Also I would not have Aviella.'

'But——' Clo began.

'I will not. Leaving no choice, Clo, the same as for you.'

'I have the choice of going to the Australian Embassy.'

... 'Good morning,' Clo heard herself stammering at the Embassy, 'can you help me? I'm a fellow member of the Australian nation, I left there twenty years ago ...'

She sighed. 'No, I have very little choice,' she agreed.

'Then you will come? Please, please, Clo!'

'Only after I exhaust my chance of other employment,' Clo said reluctantly.

'That should be easy. You can't sew ... well, not professionally ... type, fix hair.'

'Harry again, no doubt,' sighed Clo.

'Well, you two did live next door,' Isabella reminded her.

'I still have to try, Isabella. I like you, I know I said that before, but I *do*, yet I must still try, you see, I don't want to come, and that's entirely because of Tia. She might ask me ... you've said she will ... but she doesn't want me, and that's enough.'

'Would you come if there was no Tia?'

'No Tia? No Dona Juanita del Carross? Oh, yes.'

'Then there won't be, not anyway for some weeks. Tia is going back to Lisboa, but I have pretended a deep reluctance to return with her just now after my last sorowful time, and she has believed it.' Another dimple. 'You could be alone there ... well, alone with me, for those several

weeks. You could find yourself, find out what you want to
do, decide how to go about it.'

'Will the Marques be there?' asked Clo.

'He is away now. Didn't you know?'

'Yes, I knew. But afterwards, Isabella?'

'Away for an indefinite period,' said Isabella. 'When Tia
asks you, will your answer be Yes, Clo?'

'I——'

'Clo?'

'Yes,' Clo agreed, 'until I find myself.'

Not long after Isabella had left, the telephone pealed and
a cool voice asked for Senhorita Denning.

'Speaking.'

'This is Dona Juanita del Carross.'

'Yes?'

'It has occurred to me' ... oh, no, Dona Juanita, it has
been forced on you, Clo knew ... 'that the unfortunate
Condessa is in need of younger company. I have thought of
all the people I know and finally concluded that, as all the
others are tied up at this period, perhaps you might help us
out.'—Such an enthusiastic invitation, Dona Juanita,
grimaced Clo, how can I not jump for joy and accept at
once?

'I am aware that ordinarily such an offer would not
appeal to you, that now with your dear father gone, and no
immediate plans, you may have other ideas.'—I have
many other ideas, but how can they work?

'My only regret is that just now I cannot be present to
direct you' ... Clo sighed with relief at that ... 'but I will
try to make my business brief in Lisboa and to return as
soon as possible.'—By which time, Clo brightened. I can be
gone again.

'Well, *senhorita*?' persisted Dona Juanita.

'I suppose so.'

'Yes, *senhorita*?'

'Yes,' Clo said. 'Thank you.'

She put the phone down.

She had Amah bring up her bag from the basement and began to pack it. It would not take her long to empty the unit of the Denning belongings, she had been doing a little every day, and there was no need to bid any goodbyes, she could call in at any time for those.

About to fasten a last catch. Clo paused as the phone rang. The pause gave Amah the opportunity to get there first, for though, like her sister-in-law, Amah distrusted innovations, she loved the phone.

'Yes?' she asked breathlessly. 'Whatee wantee?'

Presently she put the phone down on the table. Clo had now taught her not to put it back on the receiver. She said: 'For Missy.'

Clo took it up. It was Isabella.

'Come up in half an hour, Clo,' Isabella invited.

'I'm ready now.'

'In half an hour. Sorry, I have to ring off now.' The phone at the other end went down.

Shrugging, Clo completed her catch securing, but at a more deliberate pace.

In half an hour she told Amah to go outside and hail a taxi. Then she went out of the building she had lived in for twenty years and got into the hire car.

Account Closed. She kept on thinking that as the taxi climbed the steep grade of the Peak.

At one section of the road the driver had to slacken his speed ... someone slower ahead, Clo supposed ... so that Clo had a better view of a large car bearing downward. She had seen the car before, seen the driver. In fact, she had been in it. The de Velira car. Not only did she discover this but she saw quite clearly the proud, aloof face of Dona Juanita ... and Dona Juanita saw her. The old lady looked at her quite angrily, and the anger shocked Clo. Tia might not like her, might not approve of her, might not really want her, but why was there anger there?

The moment of their eyes meeting was brief, blessedly brief for Clo. In seconds the de Velira car had sped away, and in minutes the taxi was pulling up at the Villa Serra da Estrella. Clo got out.

At once, in the warmth of Isabella's greeting, she forgot her dismay. Isabella ran out and put her arms around her, showed her the pretty room she had directed to be fixed up for her, rang for coffee to be taken to the patio.

Out there beneath the creamy temple flowers they chattered about many things ... fashion, new cosmetics, rock music, hair-styles, latest books. Then:

'When you told me to delay coming I was wondering whether you were trying to put me off,' Clo said.

'Oh, no, but I wanted Tia gone before you arrived.'

'As a matter of fact we passed each other,' Clo told her.

'Poor Tia! I do love her, really, Clo, but she—she——'

'Overwhelms?'

'That's the word. She overwhelms me.'

'But was that enough reason to get her away before I came?'

'It was. She was going to heap you with instructions concerning me.'

'You have tablets to take and she wanted me to watch that you did?' Clo suggested.

'No, I'm disgustingly healthy; I could never have fanned myself delicately as our early Portuguese gentlewomen did.'

'Then?'

'Oh,' Isabella shrugged, 'places not to go, general behaviour, all that. When you hadn't arrived by the time she had to leave, she was livid, for instead she had to write a note.'

'Where is it?' asked Clo.

'Oh, around somewhere. It wasn't important.'

'But——'

'Listen, there's the plane leaving now. You can actually hear the craft leaving the airport up here.'

'But——'

'More cake,' said Isabella. 'More coffee. The letter was quite trivial, quite fusspotty. Clo, you must take my word.'

When Isabella looked like that, Clo smiled, anyone would have taken her word. She accepted more cake, more coffee, and began, for the first time in weeks to feel young and full of life again.

They did not speak about Dona Juanita any more, except on odd occasions when Isabella would talk about her childhood, bringing in 'Tia said...' sometimes 'Tia did...' That was only to be expected, Clo knew now, for Tia had brought up all her sisters' children into adulthood.

They did a lot of things and had a lot of fun in the following two weeks. Isabella did not know Hong Kong and Clo did. On the one hand there was the bright-eyed scholar, on the other the proud teacher. Clo enjoyed showing the girl around.

They roamed round every market in Kowloon, attended the exclusive shopping palaces where styles arrived almost the moment couturiers gave them birth. They went to herbalist shops to gaze at the ancient potions and remedies, to Causeway Bay and the Tiger Balm Gardens, to a race meeting at Happy Valley.

One day they took small Tang to the Lai Chi Kok Amusement Park for a ride round the monorail, and as usual he sat quiet and remote, and when it was over had to be recalled from a long way off.

'He is an odd little boy,' said Isabella, amused. She did not seem to sense the 'difference' in Tang from other children as her aunt did, and for a few moments Clo felt a little guilty having so much of Tang while someone who loved him equally was away. She wondered about the instructions that Dona Juanita had left and Isabella had never found.

'Don't worry,' Isabella had tossed, 'all trivial and fuss-potty.'

During those two weeks, had Isabella and Harry used Tia's absence to get closer together, Clo would have felt a few qualms. But they never did. Harry lived in the annexe and the girls in the house. They even ate separately. The only times when they went out in a trio was the morning when Harry took them to the Botanical Gardens to watch the dawn shadow boxers, and another time when Harry accompanied them to the pictures. Clo had seen the films before. Her father had told her with a chuckle that they reminded him of his early youth when a movie meant either a moral pointed out or vigorous action. Cantonese films offered both. The three saw *The Fool Who Lost His Money* ... *The Attack on the Village Chen* ... and—a romantic one this time—*The Roses of Man Mo*. All in one sitting.

Then there was the celebration of Tien How, the Queen of Heaven. As a child, Clo related to her class of Harry and Isabella, little Tien How had shown miraculous power by walking over water to save her father whose junk had been overturned in a violent storm. Her birthday was celebrated now. There were lion dancers, streets bright with crackers, sword dancing ... and it was only to be expected that one of them got lost. Clo.

She found her way out, though, pleased it was her, because she knew how to get back to the villa, pleased that Harry had appreciated her bump of locality and stayed to look after Isabella.

It took some time to emerge from the crush, though, to cross to Victoria, to take the cable tram. When Clo reached there, she was glad to see that Harry's car was parked on the drive. So the pair had also found their way home.

She went into the villa, but had scarcely entered when a cold, sharp voice intercepted her.

'So this is what happens in my absence, Senhorita Denning? Tell me please what other directions of mine have you deliberately ignored?'

It was Dona Juanita, and she could not have been there very long, for she still had not unbuttoned her black gloves. Behind her, though hazily, for all her wretched attention was on Tia Juanita, stood a man. Clo sensed more than saw that he was not the Marques.

'Nothing has happened, Dona Juanita. I have ignored nothing.'

'You call this rendezvous of my niece and Professor Ferrier nothing?—No, be quiet, Blasco, I will have my say.'

For the first time Clo really looked at the man. Medium-height, modernly dressed, an attractive young-old age group and—well, nice. He smiled at Clo.

'You will go to your room, please,' snapped Dona Juanita. 'Later I will have something to say.'

'Yes, Dona Juanita.'

Clo turned and went down the hall.

CHAPTER EIGHT

CLO was surprised to hear Dona Juanita following her, following with quick, clipped steps. She wheeled round.

'The room I appointed is up the small flight of stairs.' Although the house was ranch-style and low-set, there was a variation in the levels.

'But——'

... But I was told here, brought here, Clo was about to say. She stopped herself.

'Yes? You changed it to your own choice?'

'I'll go to the room you intended.' Clo turned round again, crossed to the half flight of stairs to the room directed, and entered.

Though well furnished and large enough, the room was nothing like the room Isabella had given her. There was no floor-length window opening out to a private balcony from which one could look down on Hong Kong harbour, and it was rather a basic room.

Clo sat down on the bed, she felt so sickened she had not the heart to get up and bring her personal things along to her new background.

Presently, however, a young maid fetched everything, and when the maid had done, Dona Juanita knocked and came in.

'I'm sorry,' she apologised at once, 'I should not have done that. Perhaps you had personal reasons to change the room too much light, too much dark, too cool a breeze.'

'No.'

'Nonetheless I am sorry. Rooms do not matter.'

'But not conceding to your wishes does matter.'

The look of remorse, very faint while it had lasted, disappeared at once. 'I am after all your employer,' Dona Juanita said.

'Employer?' Clo had not thought of her time with Isabella as employment, she had thought of it as company.

'Yes, Miss Denning, you are to be paid, of course. The only reason you have not been paid so far is my absence, it was the young Condessa's wish not to have to deal with such details. Surely you did not think I asked you up here for social reasons?'

'I never thought about it,' said Clo, 'but now that I do—no, certainly you would not ask that.'

When Dona Juanita did not speak, Clo waited a bitter moment, then inquired: 'What else?'

'What else?'

'What else have I done wrongly? Not according to the list?'

'You surely are not serious, *senhorita*? You have done *nothing* according to my directions. It is almost as though you never saw my directions.' Dona Juanita looked hard at Clo, but Clo never altered her face, never flicked an eyelid. Wicked Isabella, she was thinking, she had been deliberately lying with that 'triviality' and that 'fusspottery' of hers ... all the same she would not let the old lady know of her niece's deceit.

'The room perhaps I could forgive,' resumed Dona Juanita—Forgive?—'A few other things. But your parting from the Condessa so that she and the Professor——'

'Dona Juanita, today was the first time such a thing occurred. We did become parted, as you have just accused, down at the Queen of Heaven Festival, but——'

'You took Isabella to a festival!'

'No, Harry did.' Clo saw the mistake she had made, and said quickly, 'We all went together.'

'On all occasions you went out together?'

'Isabella and I went, but not the Professor. After all he has his lectures.'

'Yet at times he went. He must have. He went today.'

'He went to the early shadow boxing in the Gardens. To the pictures.'

'The pictures!' Dona Juanita almost screamed. 'Cinemas in dark halls with close chairs.'

'The hall has to be darkened and the chairs have to be close. We saw——'

'I do not wish to know what you saw, I can well imagine it.'

'Then you'll know it was all a big laugh.'

'I do not know that,' Dona Juanita said.

After a while she resumed: 'I left a guide for you. You were to accompany the Condessa to the homes of several friends of mine to take tea, enjoy a few motoring journeys, a few inspections, perhaps a harbour cruise. Isabella wished to do some shopping, and I suggested that you accompany her there.'

'Oh, we shopped,' said Clo.

'In Victoria?'

'In Kowloon the raffish ... I mean——'

'I think I know what you mean.'

'Dona Juanita, nothing at all has happened to Isabella,' Clo assured her.

'Allow me to be judge of that. The girl to my mind is not the same as when I left her. I am sure that Blasco——'

'Blasco?' queried Clo.

'It is none of your business, Miss Denning, but Blasco Ibanez is the Portuguese gentleman I brought back with me.'

'Titled, of course.' That slipped out.

Dona Juanita looked coolly at Clo. 'Indeed so, but, like Vincente, he hides the title away.'

'On his underthings.' Fortunately Clo said that so softly it could not be heard.

'I had described poor dear Isabella to Blasco, and he was most sympathetic and anxious to comfort her. Then what do we return to? A laughing young woman on the arm ... *on the arm, senhorita* ... of a young man.

'Harry.'

'Professor Ferrier.'

'It had never happened before today ... well, only twice,' said Clo hastily.

'So you say.'

'It would mean nothing.'

'No, I don't for a moment think that Isabella would ever mean it, but how do you think it looked?'

'Looked?' Clo queried.

'Looked to Blasco Ibanez, whom I particularly brought over to——'

'Oh, no,' broke in Clo in deep shock. 'Oh, no, Dona Juanita, not that again!'

'Again?'

'Not another "arrangement", surely?'

'You are a preposterous young person!' snapped the old lady. 'Of course not. I have never done anything like that.'

'Yet Isabella did marry a Conde and is now a Condessa,' Clo pointed out.

'I will not speak on this subject. Sufficient to say that I persuaded Blasco Ibanez, whose family I know well, and whose estate has unfortunately fallen off of late, to come out and consult the Marques.'

'And if anything happens on the side, then all the better.' But again Clo kept her voice very low and to herself.

There was a silence for a while in the room. Eventually and unwillingly Dona Juanita said: 'Well, if you insist that nothing untoward has happened——'

'Nothing has happened,' Clo assured her. 'Except on

three occasions, three only, the Professor has kept to himself. Always he has dined in the annexe. Also, our market
expeditions were very quiet ones, everything we did was
very innocuous.'

'Then I suppose I must pass it over.'

'But I don't know if I can,' Clo said.

The old lady looked at her with a tinge of alarm. 'But
you would not do anything until the Marques returned?'

Clo would have given a lot to retort: 'I intend doing
something now, I intend leaving at once.' But how could
she until she had somewhere to go? money to get her there?

'I'll think it over,' she compromised.

'That is better. Here, *senhorita,* is your salary to date.
Tonight I do not wish you to dine with us.'

'Have no fear, Dona Juanita, I will not dine with you any
night.'

'Please not to be so impulsive! I said tonight because I
wish Isabella and Blasco to become acquainted with each
other tonight. Even I will dine in my own room.'

'Acquainted with V. to M.?' Once more Clo spoke under
her breath.

'You, perhaps, could dine with the Professor,' Dona
Juanita proposed.

'As you wish,' Clo shrugged.

'Then that is all ... except another matter I mentioned
in my letter. Your dress.'

'What's wrong with my dress?' demanded Clo.

'Nothing wrong, except——'

'Yes, Dona Juanita?' Surely Dona Juanita did not want
her to wear something more elaborate, that did not seem
like the old lady at all.

'It is ... well ...'

'Yes?'

'It is not a uniform.'

'A what?' asked Clo.

'I did not mean precisely uniform,' said Dona Juanita. 'But I can't think of another word to say.'

'I think you mean that modern denim does not suggest my true function?'

'Yes. Yes, in a way.'

'An entire way. What did you have in mind, a black dress, pinafore and cap?'

'A well-chosen, well-cut dress of simple design. Certainly not a flaring skirt, not a skimpy blouse.'

'Dona Juanita!' gasped Clo indignantly.

'By no means would you be attired as the other employees are, nonetheless——'

'Precisely, Dona Juanita. Nonetheless. Is there anything else?'

'Yes.' Now the old lady's voice was not just cool and disliking, it was near icy and hating. 'The child.'

'Tang.'

'He ran to me ... yes, the *pequeno* runs, he seems to have taken a liking to me ... with some unbelievable story about a—fair.'

'It's not unbelievable,' said Clo. 'Isabella and I took Tang to the children's fair.'

'He was among other children?'

'Of course.'

'In crowds?'

'Yes. But we managed a seat to ourselves on the monorail.'

'You went on that contraption?'

'Yes, Dona Juanita, we did.'

'Weren't you aware of the risk you took?'

Clo said firmly, 'Isabella loved it.'

'Not my niece, *Tang*. A small dreamy boy like that— why, he could have fallen off!'

'Oh, no, he was at the controls of it,' Clo recalled.

'Controls? ... Oh, yes, yes, I understand.'

'Do you? Do you understand, Dona Juanita?'

'Yes.'

Without another word the old lady went out.

After a few minutes Clo opened her pay packet. The contents made her blink. A few weeks of this, and she could fly out. The remuneration was more than generous. She simply must grit her teeth and abide Dona Juanita, she resolved.

She told this to Harry over dinner that night in his annexe. The servants had brought over two trays, and the pair sat at the window trying not to look across at the house proper, and the candles that were being lit in the dining room.

'Hands across the table and all that,' said Clo.

'Shut up, Clotilda!' Harry's voice was hard and worried.

'What's the matter, Harry?'

'It's not a joke, it's Isabella—And him.'

'Blasco Ibanez,' nodded Clo. 'What's it all about?'

'Your guess is as good as mine. Also the same guess, I'd say.'

'Harry, not in this year of grace.'

'Dona Juanita is still living in yesteryears, and the damnable part about it, Clo, is though Isabella laughs over it, scorns it, although she has had a modern education, *something is still there*.'

'In her?'

'Yes.'

'What?' Clo asked.

'Some deep feeling, some deep obligation. Look, it's easy for us to guffaw, but——'

'But?'

'It isn't for her.'

'But she still couldn't—she wouldn't——' Clo protested.

'She might. Tradition dies hard and all that.'

'Harry, you're taking this seriously, aren't you?'

'Very seriously,' he assured her.

'The Marques will dismiss it all in a flash.'

'... When he comes. But when is he coming? By the time that happens Isabella might be——'

'Oh, Harry, Harry!' There was silence for a moment. 'You were in earnest then, Harry, when you said that day that you didn't love me any more?'

'Yes, Clo—Clo, I love that girl.'

'She's a countess,' Clo reminded him.

'I love her,' Harry repeated.

'She's rich.'

'I love her,' he insisted.

'Dona Juanita is her aunt.'

'*I love her, Clo*, please try to understand that.'

'And—Isabella?'

'I'm sure ... I was sure ... that it's the same with her as well.'

'Then what are you worrying about?' she asked.

'That deep feeling in Isabella I just told you about, that obligation, that tradition.'

'Then if it makes a difference she can't *really* love you, and her love, anyway, wouldn't be worth one tear.'

'No? But I would still like to be a girl for a moment and cry.'

'Oh, Harry dear!'

The next day Dona Juanita sent for Clo. Clo followed the maid to the old lady's room, a very austere room both in furniture and colour. It had an attached dressing room almost as large as the bedroom itself, and sitting on the floor of the dressing room surrounded with silk patterns was a polite Cantonese gentleman. He rose at once and bowed.

'This is Chung Wong,' said Dona Juanita. 'He has brought up some colours for you to choose. When you have done that we shall settle on a design, and he shall take your measurements.' She sat down.

Clo addressed herself to the Cantonese.

'Good morning, Chung Wong. I find this a little difficult. You see, I already have a dressmaker Lee Lan.'

'Yes, Lee Lan.' Chung Wong bowed again.

'He can still be your own dressmaker,' broke in Dona Juanita autocratically, 'but Chung Wong will make your dresses for here.'

'That is true,' said Chung Wong, 'strictly only for here. How otherwise when I meet Lee Lan could I look into my friend's face?'

Dona Juanita, who had been moving restlessly during the exchange, broke in: '*Senhorita*, what colours do you like?'

'What colours do *you*, Dona Juanita, it is after all for your service.'

'Then all those pastels, Chung Wong.'

'Yes,' Chung Wong beamed.

'I like a straight line, but not too straight, not too form-fitting.'

'Yes,' said Chung Wong.

'A round neck, not too low.' The old lady turned to Clo. 'Do you like a collar?'

'Yes, with the house initials embroidered on it, or should the name be written across the back?'

'Ladies?' asked Chung Wong, bewildered.

'A small collar,' said Dona Juanita through thinned lips. 'Peter Pan?'

'Yes, Peter Pan. Now I will leave you to take the measurements. I will expect the completed order at the earliest possible moment.'

'They will all be done. They will all fit. Hong Kong clothes always fit.'

'What, Dona Juanita,' dared Clo, 'will I wear till then? Apart from my denim I have only my night clothes, and, alas, each has a low neck.'

Dona Juanita nodded to the Cantonese, ignored Clo, and left the room. A young Portuguese maid was sent to remain there until the measurements were complete, then to see Clo out again.

Clo did not see Isabella all that day, and the time hung heavily on her hands. She was not at all clear as to what was expected of her by Dona Juanita. Ordinarily she would have set out for a long mind-clearing walk ... a walk on Victoria Peak must be the most wonderful, relaxing experience in the world ... but was that permitted now?

She finished up by sitting in the very lovely villa garden, watching the soft breeze turning over the cream cups of the temple flowers, watching unbelievably beautiful butterflies flutter in and out of the azalea bushes, rest on a branch of the bauhinia tree, ruffle the trembling petals of the wind-flowers.

Butterflies! That brought Tang to her mind, and Clo got up, determined to seek him out. He had not started school again since he had come to live on the Peak. Ah Seng had told her that, so he should be somewhere around the villa— unless, of course, once more he had gone off, with a fishing line but not to catch fish or a butterfly net but not to catch butterflies in his little burnt-gold hands.

About to search out Ah Seng and ask her where Second Son was, Clo heard soft voices somewhere behind a thicket of shrubs. She went quietly across, parted the leaves and looked at a very pretty picture, a picture she had seen before—a very old lady and a very young boy. The old lady was murmuring something over and over again, and the little boy, very close to her, his golden fingers playing with the rosary that as well as her collaret of gems Dona Juanita always wore, following the movement of her faded lips with his own fresh pink lips.

'*Bom dias*,' mouthed Dona Juanita. '*Boa tarde.*'

Good gracious, she was teaching little Tang Portuguese!

No wonder, thought Clo, when she had questioned Ah Seng as to why Tang had not returned to school yet, that Amah had simply shrugged. Dona Juanita must have told Tang's mother that there was no need for him to go, that she would teach him herself. But this was absurd; school was not just for lessons, it was for friendship, for physical prowess, for healthy competition as well.

Indignantly Clo parted more bushes and walked through.

At once Dona Juanita looked up coldly. 'You interrupt. What is it?'

Clo, for all her disapproval, had the sense not to speak out in front of the child.

'Tang, go and pick up some temple flowers for the table.' The frangipanni dropped its petals unceasingly, often the lawn was more cream than green with its fallen blossom.

'Tang——' began Dona Juanita, but already the small boy had gone. As he ran off, Clo saw that he had been dressed up in a very fetching little Portuguese peasant suit, embroidered jacket, small matching shorts, long socks. This was going too far!

'Dona Juanita, you have no right to take over Tang like this!'

'His teacher has asked that he does not join classes until next term, mid-term being an inconvenient time for both instructor and scholar.'

'So you've taken over?' demanded Clo.

'For the interval until he commences again, yes.'

'You were teaching him Portuguese.'

'Good day ... good afternoon ... several similar things. Why not?'

Why not? Clo could think of many reasons why not, the most important of all that Tang should first be mastering his own language, which included Hunan as well as Cantonese, and often Shanghaiese, even some Mandarin.

Besides all that, there was his ridiculous suit.

'He is proud of it.' Clo must have spoken her objections aloud, for Dona Juanita had rushed in with a defence. 'He will not take it off. I only bought it for him to show him how little boys once dressed in old Lisboa, and he put it on at once.'

'Dona Juanita, Ah Seng and Second Son came up here with the Professor,' began Clo.

'Yes.'

'If the Professor left they would leave as well. They are not *your* property.'

'A young man like Professor Ferrier would not want to take them.'

'He might ... if he were setting up house.'

'Setting up house——?' The old lady turned sharply on Clo. 'He is not setting up house.'

'I didn't say he was, but the possibility could still be there. Then he *would* want them, and you could not prevent him from taking them.'

Dona Juanita had risen. Even though she was now an old lady, and shrunken with years, she towered over Clo. She must have been a very spectacular young girl.

'I see I must find something for you to do instead of filling in your time looking at people!' she snapped.

'Perhaps I could take Tang for a walk,' offered Clo.

'No, you could not. I took him myself earlier. He has had enough exercise for today. Tomorrow you can accompany Isabella again. Senhor Ibanez wishes to see as much of this part of the world as he can before Vincente arrives and finds him fitting employment, fitting for his position.'

'If there is any,' said Clo drily.

'There will be,' said Dona Juanita haughtily, and Clo thought what a very close circle this Portuguese roundabout of old nobility comprised.

She watched as Dona Juanita picked up the manual from which she had been reading to Tang and went back to the house.

The tedium of the following afternoon was broken up for Clo by the arrival of the new dresses ... uniforms ... overalls ... service symbols, call them what you will.

She unwrapped them, then marvelled, as she always had with Lee Lan's offerings, at the perfect work. They were all identical in style ... straight but not form-fitting, and with small demure collars. They were in the most delectable hues of lilac, green, blue, pink and buttercup. And they were pure silk. How many little silkworms had spun for this lot? Clo wondered. With each dress was a headband, silk again, but stiffened slightly with a cotton lining, and in the same melting colours as the dresses. Uniform, overall, or service symbol, they were still very nice, Clo had to concede.

She tried one on, and the fit was perfect. She was just pulling it over her head again when Isabella came in.

'What a day! Not once did Blasco leave my side.'

'Blasco Ibanez,' said Clo.

'Yes.'

'You should feel flattered,' Clo said drily.

'I felt bored,' shrugged Isabella. 'Oh, he's nice enough, and I have a feeling for all his attention that I bore him as much as he bores me, but—— Clo ... *Clo*, what is that?'

'What?'

'What you're either taking off or putting on—it looks like a St Hilda girl at Sunday chapel.'

'Were you a St Hilda girl?' asked Clo.

'St Ursula, and we wore blue not lilac.'

'I have blue, too.' Clo showed Isabella the collection.,

Isabella sighed. 'Tia, naturally, only Tia would do such a thing. You won't wear them, of course.'

'I will.'

Isabella considered this a moment, then nodded sadly. 'That's Tia for you—you see her total unfairness, but you still let her get away with it.'

'Away with what, Isabella?' Clo asked shrewdly.

'Well, in your case these badges of office.'

'I am asking you *your* case.'

'Away with—with——' Suddenly Isabella hunched her shoulders in defeat. 'I'm full of bravado away from Tia,' she confided miserably, 'but once I'm with her I go to jelly. I know you will never understand that, understand that for all one's anger against her, awe comes into it, too, for the simple reason that a time cannot be remembered when she did not command or control. Most of all, and *this* you will *never* believe, Clo, a kind of love enters as well.'

'I can understand.' Clo was thinking of an old lady teaching a little boy Portuguese and the picture it had presented. 'But a "kind of love",' she said after a few moments, 'shouldn't spoil an entire love.'

'What do you mean?' asked Isabella, perplexed.

'I don't know, Isabella, at least I only know Harry's side.'

'Harry.' Isabella looked quickly across at Clo.

'I was talking to Harry,' Clo told her. 'I believe he loves you.'

'I love him,' Isabella admitted.

'Then?'

'Oh, Clo, don't ask me, I would only answer reckless things.'

'Reckless?' queried Clo.

'Because, when faced with Tia, I know I couldn't make them happen.'

'Isabella, you're not a child, you're a woman. You've been a wife.'

'But in name only,' sighed Isabella. 'I've often thought of that. I could have had it annulled, couldn't I?'

'Your marriage?'

'Yes, because we never were man and wife, Clo. He died almost at once. Then was the time I should have escaped, but I didn't. I let Tia consume me again as she always has, always will.'

'You're a silly girl,' said Clo severely. 'She is not consuming you now. However, I may be wrong in this, for I do feel she has Blasco Ibanez in view for you.'

'That's true. But this time I won't agree. I don't believe he will, either. We just don't click.'

'There,' Clo smiled, 'she hasn't consumed you after all—you're strong.'

'No, if I were strong I would tell her about Harry, and Clo, though I plan to, I can't.'

Clo folded up the dress she had tried on. 'I'm glad you told me how you and Senhor Ibanez feel towards each other, it makes me less wretched tagging on with you in the future. I was rather surprised when Dona Juanita suggested ... *ordered* that ... that.'

'If you knew old Portuguese nobility you would be surprised at anything else. If it wasn't you, it would have to be Tia, or—or someone. We could not, at least should not, go around alone.'

'In which case I'll come, too, I suppose.'

'Not, I trust, in your St Hilda outfit,' smiled Isabella.

'That is for house duty,' said Clo. 'No, I'll wear my trusty denim.'

'Blasco will like that. For nobility, even decadent standard, he has very mod views. Tomorrow I thought we'd go to Macao. Tia will raise her brows, she does not think it is a "nice" place, but I still want to go.'

'I've never seen it myself,' agreed Clo eagerly. 'The Tai Loy, the Fat Shan or the Tak Shing?'

'What are they, Clo?'

'The boats that cross to Macao,' Clo explained.

'Being Blasco, I should think he'd want the hydrofoil.'

The following morning Blasco did.

They had only just boarded the craft when Isabella saw an old school friend from England, and gleefully claimed her. For the entire journey across, she and the old St Ursula girl talked animatedly together.

'Hockey, no doubt,' shrugged Blasco Ibanez with a wry smile.

'I wouldn't know,' proffered Clo.

'You're not an old St Trinian's?'

'It was St Ursula's. No, I was educated right here in Hong Kong by my father, who was a lecturer, and any other teacher on hand who had the time and the patience.'

'Which would comprise all the lecturers,' said Blasco gallantly. 'I would think they would be falling over themselves for the job. I am sure you were a very delightful little girl.'

'Why?' asked Clo.

'Because you are now a delightful young lady. Don't look so shocked, I can say these things, I am not what the English people say "spoken for".'

'Do they say that now?' Clo disbelieved. 'No, I'm not shocked. Also I knew before that anything between you and Isabella was a mislaid plan.'

'Excellent then, we both understand each other. Can't we go on from there?'

'Where, *senhor*?'

'Blasco, Clo,' he corrected.

'Blasco?'

'I like you. I did from the first moment I saw you. I am by no means rich, but on the other hand I am not as poor as Dona Juanita considers me. She keeps telling me, not directly, of course, how lucky I am with the small means I have to be a contender for the fair Isabella.'

'Oh, you Portuguese nobility!' Clo had to laugh.

'On the Ibanez account a little frayed at the edges,' Blasco admitted. He looked at Clo and brightened. 'I say, we get along pretty well, don't we?'

'I'm not committing myself.'

'Well, don't worry. I myself never worry. Here today, gone tomorrow, enjoy the life you hold in your hands. Let us now enjoy Macao.'

The hydrofoil sped past the many green islets of Hong Kong, past the villages of Lantao to the starboard, Cheung Chau to port. Blasco, who had been conferring with the guide, came back to tell Clo they were now in Communist waters.

In time they came to the line dividing the yellow depths of the Pearl River from the deep blue depths of Hong Kong. The yellow was from the sediment, Blasco told Clo the guide had said.

Some time later they reached Macao. Isabella said good-bye to her old school friend, and the trio, Isabella, Blasco and Clo, did the expected Macao things.

They had dinner in a banqueting hall, finishing the meal with Portuguese brandy instead of *shau shing* as a tribute to this tiny corner of Portugal.

They strolled the more Chinese than Portuguese, rather lackadaisical streets, enjoying the soft warm air, the cobbled alleyways, beneath them in picturesque half circle a shining, lapping bay.

Blasco was keen to try the gambling houses, so for the first time Isabella went with him alone, for she was enthusiastic, too, leaving Clo to wander around and admire the architecture with its preponderance of Baroque.

'You don't mind?' they asked.

'I never win anything.'

'But the fun?'

'More fun for me here,' Clo assured them. 'I'll see you in an hour.'

'Unless,' grinned Blasco, 'we strike a run of luck. Then we won't budge!'

Clo watched a mah-jongg game played on the side walk, but so near to the street that cars had to edge by; she took a taxi to where she could look across to impassive-faced sentries with red stars on their caps looking back at her over a strip of neutral territory. She returned, asking the driver about the Street of Eternal Felicity.

'No, *senhorita*,' the man, rather proper, very wrinkled, advised, 'no.'

'Then the Posada de Macao, perhaps?'

'Ah, yes. Coffee, *senhorita*?'

'Please.'

As she paid the man, Clo smiled a little in memory, wondering what had changed Dona Juanita to allow Isabella to have come to this *not* 'nice' place. But then Blasco had happened, of course.

She went into a coffee garden, still smiling, and sat in a cobbled courtyard under a tree. Now was the time, she was musing, remembering Vincente, to hold all summer in your hand, to drift off to sleep to the whirr of little insects, to the twitter of bulbul birds, to the clop of wooden pattens . . .

'But it must be a wine drift, not a coffee drift,' a voice said at Clo's elbow. 'Coffee alerts. Wines bring dreams.'

Not far from dreams, even though she had been drinking coffee not wine, Clo opened her eyes.

The Marques was snapping his fingers for another chair on the other side of the small table. He was calling for a long slender bottle of rosé wine, two long slender glasses.

'Well, *pequena*,' he asked after the wine had come, been poured and they had touched glasses. 'Well, my little one?'

CHAPTER NINE

'YOU'RE in England!' disbelieved Clo.

'I am here.' A challenging smile. 'Touch me.'

Clo lowered her gaze, ostensibly to see that her faintly-trembling hands ... why were those wretched fingers shaking? ... took a good grasp of the slender neck of the glass, but really to elude a dark, warm glance.

The Marques gave her several minutes to do so, to touch him as he had invited to assure herself he was real, then he shrugged and explained: 'I flew from England last night, arrived in the early hours, reached the Villa Serra da Estrella not long after you had left.'

'So you followed us.'

Another shrug. 'Macao is a place where I do big business, I had to come regardless, but I must admit to being curious.'

'Curious?' she echoed.

'As to why my respected Tia who does not consider Macao "nice" was agreeable to let Isabella make the journey across. But then, of course, she had you as a duena— *And* there was young Ibanez.'

'Oh, yes, Blasco.'

'So it is Blasco, is it?'

'Well, I could hardly call him Senhor Ibanez all the time,' said Clo defensively.

'And he, what does he call you?'

'You're being ridiculous!'

'I see,' said the Marques drily. He refilled his glass from the slender bottle.

'I don't think,' he said presently, 'Tia had this in view.'

'What are you talking about?' she asked.

'A marriage arrangement that goes astray. Oh, Tia never said it was a marriage arrangement, Blasco was simply the son of a dear friend of hers who had come on less fortunate times, so perhaps I could suggest something, and in the meantime he would be company for Isabella.'

'With V. to M.' This time Clo did say it aloud.

'Exactly. But has it come off instead with the—*duena*?'

'I'm not a *duena*,' Clo assured him.

'Agreed, a *duena* would not call Senhor Ibanez Blasco.'

'The person we are speaking about is not with me now, is he?' Clo looked indicatively around her.

'No,' nodded Vincente, 'but I could guess where he is, having previously known the family Ibanez. No doubt at the roulette table.'

'Yes. With Isabella.'

'Then she also will be entranced, especially with the win she will make.'

'How do you know?' asked Clo.

'My child, that is the rule of the house, all Macao gambling houses—a little encouraging win in the beginning.' He smiled and spread his hands.

'Well, now do you believe I'm not trying to come between two young lovers?' Clo demanded.

'Who are not lovers?' he parried back.

'Quite right. They take no notice of each other.'

' "The best-made plans——" ' he quoted.

'A Portuguese knows Robert Burns?'

'Yes, but the Portuguese would sooner quote Elizabeth Barrett Browning's Sonnets. *Sonnets from the Portuguese* —didn't you know?'

'I'll take your word for it.' Again Clo evaded that warm dark glance.

'So Blasco is pursuing you and not my cousin?' Vincente asked presently.

'He's doing nothing of the sort!' she denied crossly.

'But he does like you and you like him?'

'We struck up a friendship at once,' Clo admitted. 'Hadn't you better see to your Macao business, Marques, or are you intending to stay over?'

'I've already concluded my business, concluded it very satisfactorily,' he told her, 'and no, I am not staying over. I have come to take you three children back.'

'We're booked on the hydrofoil,' Clo told him.

'It will be cancelled. You will travel in my yacht.'

'Your yacht will be no novelty,' Clo said unkindly, 'we saw everything on the way over.'

'Ah, but you will not be going the same way back.'

'Is there another way?' she asked.

'Round several small islands that you did not see before.' A pause. 'One of them mine.'

'Yours?'

'Do not sound so impressed, Clotilda, it is a very small island—an islet.'

'And you have a house on it?'

'Well, I don't change to Robinson Crusoe and sleep in a cave,' he drawled.

'Won't it take longer going that way?'

'Certainly.'

'Then we'll be arriving at Hong Kong late at night?'

'No'

'No?' she questioned.

'No, because we will stay the night on my small islet, my Villa das Flores.'

'Has it flowers?'

'Ah——' he smiled.

Clo said tentatively: 'I don't think Isabella will agree. I think she'll want to go home.'

'You mean there would be more attraction there than at a villa of flowers, a romantic islet?'

'Is it romantic?' she asked.

'You will see for yourself.'

'I asked you, Marques. Has romance come there for you?'—Clo wondered what had taken possession of her to talk to him like this.

'You pose too many questions,' Vincente drawled.

'And receive no replies. But' ... hastily ... 'I'm not really interested. I mean, *senhor*, of course we couldn't go, we all only came over in what we wear.'

'In my small yacht there are three valises, packed under the direction of Tia Juanita. Blasco's, Isabella's ... yours.'

'You mean you actually persuaded Dona Juanita to send over what would be needed?' asked Clo incredulously.

'It needed little persuasion,' he assured her, 'not with Blasco Ibanez one of the party.'

'Well, I still don't think——'

'Have you seen any of these small islets between Macao and Hong Kong before?' he demanded.

'No.'

'But you would like to see them? See one?'

'Yes. Yes, I would. But Isabella——'

'Isabella is beaten three to one. You wish to go to my islet, Blasco will wish to go, I wish to go, and Isabella——' He spread his hands significantly. Presently he asked carefully:

'How goes it with Isabella and Professor Ferrier?'

Clo answered simply: 'They love each other, I think.'

'You *think*?'

'That is my reply. You see, I can't understand why, if Isabella really does love Harry, she doesn't—why she doesn't——'

'Yes?'

'Declare herself. Go to his side.'

'You would do that?' he queried.

'Oh, yes! I don't believe in only going halfway to the man you love, I believe in——'

'Yes?'

'In going the whole way, *senhor*.' Clo bit her lip. The last thing she wanted to do was delve deep like this. To cover her embarrassment, an embarrassment caused by his warm black gaze on her, she asked: 'How did you know you would find me here?'

'I knew it would be the Posada de Macao,' he said calmly.

'Knew?'

'Your eyes and lips followed me when I spoke of it that time.'

'It might have been the Street of Eternal Felicity,' she suggested.

'Oh, no, little Quaker, not you,' he said gently.

'Why do you call me that?' she demanded crossly.

'Because you are still the acorn, I always think.'

'You said I was a tree one night.'

'For that night only. Like Cinderella returned to her pumpkin, you returned to your acorn after midnight. You are young and untried, Clotilda.' He added: 'Still.'

'You don't say how you found me,' Clo persisted.

'I looked in at every wayside café.'

'That would take a long time,' she commented.

'No, I chose only the ones where you could hear the whirr of small insects, the twitter of bulbul birds, the clop of pattens.'

'All summer in your hand,' Clo murmured.

'Time standing still,' he said.

With an effort Clo stirred herself. 'Time has obviously not stood still for Isabella and Blasco.' She indicated the returning couple. 'They look more frazzled than they did before they went to the gambling house.'

'Frazzled?' the Marques frowned.

'Not so confident, not so composed.'

'No, a few losses bring that.' He stood up and signalled the other pair, and soon the table for two was a table for four.

They both had parted with their money, as Vincente had said, they had started off winning, then they had begun to go down.

'Now we will go home,' Isabella pouted. 'Vincente, why are you here?'

'*Not* to take you home, *pequena,* but to my small islet.'

'But I wish to go home!'

'Nonetheless you will come to the islet.'

'I will not. Tia Juanita would not like it.'

'Tia has packed a bag,' he said calmly.

Now Isabella was positively thunderous. She tried some more objections to no avail, especially when Blasco expressed enthusiasm.

They finished another bottle of the Portuguese rosé, then found their way to a pretty go-down, a cutting in a bank of a small deep stream that flowed in from the sea and that had provided a safe harbourage for Vincente's yacht.

'Your bag is stowed inside, Isabella, please stow yourself as well.' Vincente called a young man who was waiting by the go-down, and the young man took over and in minutes they were leaving the cutting, leaving the stream and dipping up and down in the ocean.

The crossing, a crossing much briefer than the morning's since the islet was exactly halfway between Hong Kong and Macao, was as smooth as their earlier journey. The Marques told Clo that there was seldom any roll, except at the height of the north-east monsoon.

'Why did you call your yacht *Kurpinta*?' Clo asked.

'An Australian asks that? Ah, but you are away from your country many years.'

'Nearly all my life,' she admitted.

'Then for an answer you must ask Harry. It means Rainbow After Rain, and was the name of one of his waif homes. His favourite home.'

'Poor Harry!' sighed Clo.

'Yes, but he seems to have had no sad result, only a happy one.'

'Happy, yes,' she agreed, 'but not a home still. That was why he was so eager to leave the hotel.'

'And now you tell me it is no home up at the Villa Serra da Estrella?'

'I don't think it is for Harry.' Clo turned away, and in doing so turned to Blasco, who had evidently deposited the cross Isabella below and come to seek out more pleasant company. Out of the corner of her eye Clo saw Vincente shrug, then turn his attention to his boat.

The yacht, not large, but sparkling white, with a lissom line and an amazing efficiency, made the journey a delight. Clo was sorry at first when she saw the tiny islet presenting itself, she could have kept on and on ... and then she drew her breath in enchantment. The scene before her looked like the pictures sometimes painted on black velvet cushions, too lovely to be real. Yet this *was* real. It seemed a faerie place, lilac-misted, dreamlike, until you came near enough to see its trees and rocks and crescent beaches ... and a house.

'The Villa das Flores,' Vincente, beside Clo, said.

Clo whispered: 'The house of flowers.'

There was a little white jetty and an adjoining boathouse, and a man was waiting to help with the mooring. Between the four of them, the man, Vincente's skipper, Blasco and the Marques, the *Kurpinta* was soon tied up and its passengers taken off.

A flagged path led up to the villa, which had been positioned in the middle of the island. It was built of white timber ... timber for easier transport, Vincente said ... but had many Gothic touches that one rather would have associated with stone. But the arches were stone, and gathered from the islet, and so were the cool terraces, the courtyards, fountains and flower pots trailing blossoms.

'It's lovely,' Clo said. 'It really is a place of flowers. Aubretias, portulacas, veronicas and our own windflowers.'

Isabella did not comment. She had plenty to say in the room the girls were given a few minutes later, though.

Really, she pouted, Vincente was the utter end! She had not wanted to come. She had no doubt that Tia had packed all the wrong things. She believed she was catching a chill. What would Harry think?

'Dona Juanita will tell him, Isabella,' Clo assured her.

'Tell him what? Don't answer—I know. She will tell Harry I have preferred to delay my return, that I am on the islet—with Blasco.'

'And the Marques and me,' Clo pointed out reasonably.

'She'll leave that out.'

'Then when you return you can tell him yourself.'

'He won't be there.'

'Of course he will.'

'No, he won't, Clo, he will have left. You see, for all his pleasant nature, Harry is—is——'

'Strong?'

'Yes. He has told me I must make up my mind.'

'And haven't you?' asked Clo.

'Oh, yes, yes ... but I can't seem to find the courage to say it. I'd say it now if Tia were here, but she's not, and tomorrow I'll be cowardly again.'

'Well, it's all up to you Isabella,' Clo sighed.

When the girls went to the dining alcove for the evening meal, Vincente had had a chicken pilaff prepared. He had mixed the salad himself.

Clo ate with relish, but Isabella pushed hers aside with disinterest. A chill coming, as she had said? Or was she still wishing she could see Dona Juanita face to face *now*?

Clo was not to think about that during the evening that followed, an evening shared with Vincente and Blasco, for Isabella had gone straight to their room ... but she did think about it in the morning. She awoke early and stretched and yawned and looked to the other twin bed. It was empty. Isabella had slept in it last night—Clo had tiptoed over to replace a discarded rug before she went to bed herself but she had left it now. At home she was anything but an early riser, yet it was only five o'clock and Isabella was gone.

Clo leapt out and not even stopping to pull over a robe she ran to the patio.

The swimming pool, perhaps, she thought. Isabella must have wakened, felt better and decided on a rousing splash.

Clo raced across the dewy lawns in her bare feet. No, the pool lay blue and inviting, but it also lay empty.

The gardens, then? She did every inch of the gardens, thinking as she walked that the place only needed a strutting peacock or two to complete a perfect picture.

No Isabella.

The beaches? There were only a few, the rest of the tiny coast was just rocks.

No one was there.

Clo now took a look at *Kurpinta*, at Rainbow After Rain. It was as lissom as ever, and as complete ... and yet——

Why, the dinghy was missing. Oh, that utter idiot of a girl! She had told Clo she would have liked to have confronted Tia now, but surely, even though the islet was nearer to Hong Kong than Macao was, she had not ... had not ...

Clo came closer, checked for oars and saw, too, that they were missing. Then she turned and raced back to the house.

Before she could reach the villa, Vincente came racing down to meet her. He was dressed in bathing trunks, and must have been on his way for an early swim when her anxious cries had halted him.

'What in heaven is it, Clotilda?' he demanded.

'Isabella,' she panted. 'She wasn't in her bed when I wakened, so I ran out to look.'

'Like that?' He was frowning at Clo in her skimpy pink nightie. 'You will catch a cold. Here!' He put a very large, fluffy towel he carried around her.

'Don't fuss over me, Vincente, find Isabella!' Clo almost shouted.

'Oh, I will, don't worry, and I'll reprimand her, alarming you like this.'

'Vincente, *you* have to be alarmed, too. I think Isabella has taken the dinghy.'

'What?' he snapped.

'The dinghy has gone. And the oars.'

'*Uno momento*, Clo, let me have this clearly. The dinghy has gone? Isabella has gone?'

'Yes. Yes!'

'Then wait here,' he said, and his voice was rough with concern . . . and something else. Anger.

I wouldn't be Isabella when he finds her, Clo shivered. Then she thought anxiously, if she is found.

Isabella was found, of course. Vincente and his man got out a small runabout and found her on the other side of the islet. No, she was not trying to row to Hong Kong. No, she was not trying to return to Macao. Vincente related this to Clo an hour later. Isabella was in her room crying.

'You were stern with her,' Clo accused.

'I could have whipped her! The little fool, unknowingly I'll admit, was approaching Communist waters. Yes, that is so. Nothing would have happened, but she had no right to be where she was.'

'What was she doing?' asked Clo.

'Just rowing around,' he said.

'Why?'

'You know why as well as I do, because she is an abject coward. She knows what she wants, but she can't face up to Tia, the spineless child.'

'Vincente, don't speak like that,' Clo begged.

'How, then?'

'Comfort her.'

He frowned. 'Oh, no.'

'Then encourage her. Tell her what to do.'

'No again, Clotilda, in a case like this she must make up her own mind. She must come, not just halfway, as a certain person told me' ... again that warm dark gaze ... 'but the whole way.'

'It mightn't be easy,' Clo defended her.

'Love never is.'

'You could still help her,' she insisted.

'Tell me this, *senhorita*, would you need help?'

'I ... well ... I think ... I mean ...'

What Clo would have answered, she did not know, and Vincente was not to know, either. Blasco had joined them, his dark melting eyes instantly sending liquid messages to Clo.

A little intoxicated with their complimentary messages ... who wouldn't have been? ... Clo accepted Blasco's invitation to walk between the flowers.

'Not long,' called the Marques rather harshly, 'we leave for home almost at once.'

It was a silent journey across to Hong Kong. The sea was still as calm and the little islets still sparkled like gems in a necklace, but Isabella was withdrawn, Blasco plainly piqued at having so little time with Clo, Vincente brooding, and Clo ... well, Clo felt distinctly apprehensive. Apprehensive for Isabella, for herself, though she could not have said why, to her mind she had done no wrong, apprehensive for everybody, even little Tang.

'You are a female Sinbad,' Vincente said once, emerging from his own introspection to glower at Clo, 'you carry the old man of the sea on your shoulders.'

'Out here it would scarcely be an old man from anywhere else,' she shrugged.

'Very clever. Here is Victoria Hong Kong side now.'

In a few minutes they were moored, and being borne by Vincente's car, which he had left parked by the boathouse, up to the Villa Serra da Estrella. Isabella at once retired to her room, Vincente took Blasco out with him to examine some new project he had in mind, so Clo, correctly if un-enthusiastically, sought out Dona Juanita. When she could not find her, she asked her maid. The maid informed Clo that Dona Juanita had taken the small boy Tang to the doctor.

'The doctor?' queried Clo. 'Is he ill?'

'The Senhora thought he seemed not as active as he should be.'

'Where did she take him?'

'A Portuguese doctor she knows.' The woman, Portuguese herself, gave the slightest of shrugs, but for all its slightness Clo picked on it.

'Don't you like this doctor?' she demanded.

'Oh, yes, but——'

'But?'

'He is not young—in fact quite old. I myself would prefer a younger person. There are so many new ideas. But of course' ... eyes down ... 'that is my opinion, and the *senhorita* would never mention my preference.'

'Certainly not, Maria.'

Clo turned and went and found Ah Seng.

'What is wrong with Second Son, Amah?' she asked anxiously.

'Nothing, nothing. Just a little tired sometimes.' Ah Seng made a sleepy gesture with her head sidewise on her two folded hands.

'Then why did Dona Juanita take him to the doctor?'

'Because she love Tang,' Ah Seng said.

'*I* love Tang.'

'All love Second Son,' agreed Amah equably. 'I make little sugar bun for him for when he come home.'

Clo wandered away again. She felt vaguely unsettled. She kept picking up things, then putting them down. She wished that Isabella was not being so uncommunicative; she wished Harry was there, but Harry would be at lectures and not home for hours. She wondered how long the men would be.

It was Dona Juanita and Tang who arrived first, Tang with a clockwork toy Tia had bought him which he could not wait to show his mother.

'What's wrong with him?' Clo asked as soon as he had gone. She was aware she asked it abruptly, but she could not help herself.

Dona Juanita raised disapproving brows, disapproving Clo's forthrightness.

'My old friend thinks perhaps a small blood disorder. He has prescribed a tonic for Tang.'

'But you don't "think" these days, Dona Juanita—I mean, not medically.'

'Doctor Montales is a very respected old physician.'

'But still old,' pointed out Clo.

'Yes, old, painstaking, steady, not like the young, slap-dash medicos of today.'

'The world has changed, and with it have the doctors. If they haven't, then they should not be practising.'

'You are criticising Doctor Montales?' demanded the old lady.

'Never, but if Tang is ill——'

'He is not ill. But neither is he as bright as I would like.'

'And *I* would like,' insisted Clo. 'I am in this, too, Dona Juanita. I have more right to him, remember. We—my father and I—employed his mother long before Harry did. You never actually employed Ah Seng at all, she just came along with Tang.'

'While the child is under my roof I am responsible for him,' Dona Juanita insisted.

'The *Marques*'s roof.'

The old lady closed her eyes at that. Closed her lips as well.

'So you took him to an old-fashioned doctor.' Clo knew she probably was being very unfair, but she could not help herself.

'Miss Denning, you overstep yourself. Also, why are you here? I believed that Vincente would prolong the excursion.'

'Isabella wished to return,' Clo explained.

'Why? Did anything go wrong?'

'Nothing,' lied Clo, feeling a lie was the easiest way out.

Dona Juanita asked outwardly matter-of-factly but actually very awarely, Clo knew:

'And the Condessa and Senhor Ibanez?'

'No way.' Clo had not intended slang, but her reply came out like that.

'*You* saw to that, I think,' snapped the old lady.

'I?'

'Look at you. In a flimsy—and revealing—dress! Sandals! And what have you in your hair?'

Too late Clo realised that the hibiscus Blasco had plucked on their brief walk at the Villa das Flores and tucked over her appropriate ear—appropriate, he had teased, for a now betrothed girl—still nestled there. She put up her hand and self-consciously touched it.

'So,' said Dona Juanita, 'you and Blasco——'

'No,' said Clo firmly.

'Then certainly not you and my nephew. Oh, no, Vincente would have more perception than that.'

'You mean than a flower plucked at random and placed in someone's hair.'

'*Your* hair. Also, you are not wearing one of the dresses I had made for you.'

'I've only just returned,' Clo pointed out.

'Then change at once, *senhorita*.'

'To my badge of office?'

'Also do something about your hair.'

'Cut it off?' Clo said angrily.

'You are an impertinent girl, you know I meant to re-move that ridiculous flower.'

'Yes, Dona Juanita.' Clo paused. 'I'm sorry I have offended. I'm sorry also about Doctor Montales—no doubt he's very good, but I really am as concerned as you.'

'Please go.' The old lady had turned away.

Her ungraciousness undid any understanding that Clo was prepared to offer her senior. By the time she reached her room she was in a fine rage.

She took off her own dress and put on one of the uniform dresses ... not pink, too feminine, not blue, too senti-mental, not mauve, too—— Yellow would do. Clear, un-cluttered, perceptive yellow.

The headbands had been a bonus from the dressmaker, they had never been ordered by Dona Juanita, but now Clo took a malicious pleasure in damping and combing very *very* straight her fine acorn hair, pulling tightly over it the matching yellow band.

I only need to curtsey, she thought, looking at herself in the mirror, I only need to bow.

In her absorption she had not heard a car arrive back at the villa, had not heard Vincente and Blasco come into the hall. Tilting her chin, setting her mouth, Clo left her room and descended the few steps to the entrance level.

The rest seemed like a tableau.

At one end of the hall was Tia Juanita, who evidently,

unlike Clo, had heard the men's arrival and come out to greet them. Halfway along was Blasco, turning now to Clo. At the doorway, barely in the hall, was Vincente, and he was already facing her.

For a full minute the tableau was played, not a movement by anybody. Then the Marques broke the silence, broke the spell quite violently.

'What in Christopher do you think you are playing at?' he fairly shouted at Clo. 'Why are you dressed like that? What tomfoolery is this? Take off that absurd headgear at once! Go in and remove that ridiculous serving dress. Then come to me and tell me why, why, *why*? Do you hear me?'

'Yes, *senhor*, I hear you.' Clo said no more.

She scuttled back to her room and closed the door.

CHAPTER ELEVEN

VINCENTE rang for two dinners to be brought to his study.

'I can't eat,' Clo said when the maid had left.

'You will eat, though, you will eat for strength, Clotilda, for strength will be needed in your next few weeks.'

'How few?' she asked sadly.

'How can one tell? How does a little wind know when it stirs itself how many flowers it will break from a stem?'

'Why Tang?' she almost wept. 'Why? Why?'

'Why not Tang? Why any other son? any daughter? No one knows these things.'

'Can't anything be done, anything at all?'

'Only what Tang already has in plenty: loving kindness.'

'He's too little,' she muttered.

'But every inch of that littleness a fine man.'

'It's not fair!'

'No, it's not fair,' Vincente said unexpectedly, unexpected by Clo, and he said it in a cracked voice. After his previous reasoning with her this agreement broke Clo up. She began to cry, staccato little-girl crying, nothing held back, and Vincente did not stop her.

Eventually there were no tears left, and she looked at the Marques dry and hollow-eyed.

'As I brought the small one back I did a lot of thinking, Clotilda,' he said.

'Yes?'

'The obvious, the only way is to let life go on the same.'

'You mean as it's going now?' she queried.

'Yes.'

Out of the corner of her eye she could see Dona Juanita moving instinctively forward, then, more slowly, retreating again.

'So,' the Marques said again. 'Very well then, don't let it occur another time.'

'You don't mind this mode of apparel, then?' Clo glanced down at herself.

'Those simple clothes *are* you, *senhorita*.'

'And a flimsy dress, a hibiscus placed behind the ear?'

'It all depends on which one has placed the flower.'

Now any humbleness in Dona Juanita, any gratefulness for covering up for her, was gone. The old lady's head was held high in her customary aristocratic, faintly arrogant manner. She turned and went back to her sitting room, while Vincente watched her with amusement.

'Do you know what,' he smiled, 'I really don't think Tia minded that abject dress.'

Clo did not answer.

'*Senhorita*, I spoke to you.'

Clo looked at him, saw the faintest beginnings of a suspicion there, so killed it at once by asking:

'What do I do with those clothes?'

'Give them to Ah Seng.'

'She always wears Amah tunics.'

'Then to her sisters, cousins, aunts, so long as I am not troubled by them any more.'

'Were you troubled, *senhor*?' she asked.

'No, perhaps that is not the right word. I was displeased.'

'Then your displeasure is over,' she told him. 'I'll give the clothes away.'

'Thank you ... but some displeasure still persists. I'm speaking now of the other adornment you wore.'

'Adornment?' she said, puzzled.

'The matter of a hibiscus flower behind your ear. I may be a business man, but I am still aware of its message.'

'It was only in fun,' Clo protested.

'Many a true word is spoken in jest—I learned that at English school. Yes, I will certainly speak to Ibanez.'

'To Blasco?' she gasped. 'Are you quite mad?'

'He did not tuck in that blossom, then?'

It was a temptation to lie again, but Clo fought against it. She had lied enough for today.

'Yes,' she said directly, 'Blasco did it. Is that such a heinous sin?'

'Not on Blasco's part, for I do believe that for him it was just a pleasant dalliance. But for you——'

'Yes, *senhor*?'

'For you, *pequena*, it was the last frantic beating of foolish wings against a window.'

'Foolish?' she queried.

'The little bird believed it knew what it wanted. The little bird was wrong.'

'But it still beat.'

'To no avail. *To no avail*, Clotilda.' Now the black warm gaze was holding Clo. In spite of herself, a little mesmerised, Clo made a half step forward. She heard him laugh softly and deeply, and despised herself for that instinctive move forward. She cleared her throat to tell this arrogant man what she thought of him, but the Marques had gone.

Before Clo could return to her room, Dona Juanita emerged from her boudoir again.

'*Senhorita!*' she called.

'Yes, Dona Juanita?'

'I wish to thank you for your silence just now.' The old, thinned lips barely mouthed the thanks.

'That's all right, *senhora*,' said Clo flatly.

'It is not for me. I do not need your help,' the old lady went on.

'I didn't give it in that spirit.'

'Perhaps not, in which case we will forget it. I am just mentioning it now as I want you to realise I am afraid of nothing and nobody, and particularly of my nephew whom I brought up from a small child in nappies.'

A quirk took possession of Clo, it was all she could do not to giggle out loud. Somehow she could not, and never would, picture the grand Marques as a child in nappies.

'I'm glad you dread nothing,' she said instead. 'I myself harbour many fears. One of them is Tang.' She said it just for something to retort, but even as she uttered it, she was sharply aware, as she had been aware at other odd times, of a finger touching her heart, touching it harshly because of a little deep-gold boy.

'Tang?' The old lady's voice came like a rapier.

'Yes. You saw fit to take him to a doctor.'

'A disorder of the blood—I told you.'

'But I'm not satisfied, Dona Juanita,' Clo said firmly.

'Then you must ask my physician, mustn't you, Miss Denning. You must ask Doctor Montales.' Dona Juanita swept proudly back to her room.

... No, I won't do that, Clo knew, but I will ask someone else.

But whom to ask? Clo had had no need to consult a doctor herself, and Dad had kept any such visits strictly private; she had not the slightest idea of where to go.

She asked Harry that night, a nervously happy Harry, barely hearing Clo's questions, anxious only to talk about Isabella and himself.

'She's going to speak to her aunt as soon as she has an opportunity. I can hardly believe it,' he mused happily. 'I knew she loved me, but I never thought she would make the essential forward step.'

'I want a doctor, Harry—a good one,' interrupted Clo urgently.

'I've been offered a post in Honolulu, under the same

bequest as we're under here. It's a similar endowment, a similar set-up. Isabella will love Honolulu.'

'The name of a good doctor, Harry!' she urged.

'It will be expensive for us, I suppose, but we'll cope. Also, Isabella will have to become accustomed to living in far less luxurious surroundings. We'll be in a similar hall of residence to what you were, Clo.'

'But Isabella has her own money.' For a moment Clo forgot about the doctor.

'It has been left to Isabella, but only on the judgement of her aunt,' he told her.

'But a wife is entitled on her own account.'

'Under our law, yes, and eventually under their law as well, but a waiting period can be insisted upon by the executor, and the executor in this instance is Tia Juanita. In which case...' Harry gave a rueful shrug. 'But Isabella is still adamant,' he continued. 'She says she would forgo any money for ever, not just a certain period of years, to be with me.'

'That's wonderful, Harry! Now, Harry, a doctor.'

'Try out the new Grandling Clinic, Clo, there's a panel of young, keen American medics there, all as up to date as tomorrow.' Harry wrote down an address.

As though Tia had been overhearing the conversation and had dug in her toes, Clo barely saw Tang during the next few days. Always Tia had something arranged for him —a ride with her in the chauffeured car, a visit to a friend's where no doubt she showed off the lovely sunflower child. The only time when Clo could corner him was when he arrived home again from the outing, naturally a little fatigued after it all, so that the downward curve of his exquisite little mouth was only to be expected, the frequent brush of his thick dark lashes on his golden cheeks a normal thing.

Several times Clo thought of asking Vincente, but Vincente was very busy these days; he was planning a large takeover, Blasco reported.

Blasco was not 'in' the firm yet, but hoped to be. He said that Vincente had been impressed with him, but also that the Marques was a bit of a hard nut.

'Big businessmen have to be,' Clo told him. 'One day you'll be one yourself.'

'I expect so, but until that time comes, let's get around, Clo.'

'Tia——' she began.

'Must have got the message by now, especially with the Professor strutting around like the cat who got the cream.'

'Something tells me, Blasco, that like Isabella and Vincente, you also were English-schooled,' Clo commented.

'Yes,' Blasco grinned. 'Tomorrow, Clo?'

'I don't know,' she sighed. 'Harry might look happy, but Tia is looking more formidable than ever.'

'Sticks and stones—that's something else I learned at English school.'

Because she was never tired of Hong Kong, of Kowloon the raffish, Clo agreed. They did all the Hong Kong things, the Markets, the New Territories, the beaches, the theatres, and were eating in the floating restaurant at Aberdeen when Aviella Martinez strolled along. Aviella, thought Clo, had a talent for appearing in select restaurants, but after all you would not expect to find a gilded girl like her in the middle of a bargain alley.

Aviella was not so brittle today. Evidently she had given up the idea of living in the Villa Serra da Estrella, of associating herself with Vincente, for she greeted Clo quite amiably—Perhaps, thought Clo, it was because Blasco was with her, for certainly Blasco was no naïve Harry.

She looked more beautifully elegant than ever, and instinctively Clo glanced down at herself. Although the Marques might like simplicity, she had a fair idea that

Blasco did not. On several occasions he had flashed her rather rueful looks, she had thought, and he always was wonderfully impeccable himself.

'Senhorita Aviella Martinez,' Clo murmured now, 'Senhor Blasco Ibanez.'

Blasco, bowing, said: 'I know the family well.'

'I know yours.'

It all went on from there.

They ate together, Clo choosing Beggar's Chicken because she still could not bear to indicate to a waiter which silver-swishing fish she fancied and she told the other two about the beggar of old Hangchow who stole a chicken and concealed it in lotus leaves and then pond mud, and how, when cooked by mistake, it had turned out like this ... at least she told them until she saw they were not attending. They were looking at each other, and they kept on looking after the meal had finished until the waiter coughed discreetly and suggested the lounge.

There the looks started all over again, until Clo, glancing at her watch, said that she must leave. Neither Aviella nor Blasco moved. Clo suggested then that she go on, see Senhorita Martinez some day in the future, perhaps she would come up to the villa? Yes, Aviella would do that, and no, dear Senhorita Denning, please not to be disturbed at having to go.

Clo went.

Back in town, she remembered the card bearing the name of the clinic that Harry had suggested, and was standing rummaging in her purse and discovering she had left it behind when a hand closed over hers.

'That is a silly thing to do, Senhorita Denning. In one second I could have your worldly possessions and be lost in the crowd. What are you doing here by yourself?' The Marques looked down on Clo, and obediently she closed her bag.

'I'm not—I mean I am now, but I came with Blasco.'

'Yes, I have been noticing the time you have spent with Ibanez. But where is he now?'

'Still at the restaurant, I think, but now the bored waiter in the lounge is making faces instead of the meal waiter, because he doesn't attempt to go.'

'What is this, Clotilda?'

'He ... Blasco ... took me there, and we ran into Aviella,' she explained.

'Oh, the beautiful Aviella.'

'Blasco thought so. Very obviously he thought so.'

'Don't tell me' ... angrily ... 'he suggested to you that you returned by yourself?'

'Oh, no, I suggested it myself,' she said hastily.

'And that pair agreed.'

'Of course. Wouldn't you have?'

'No. I would have gone with you.'

'But if I was in the position that Aviella was.'

'And I was in Blasco's position? The king's men would not have budged me. Look, we can't talk here, we are impeding the traffic. Is there any place where we can take tea?'

'Yes. Tea and Cake.'

'Tea and——'

'Tea and Cake,' she repeated. 'It was my father's favourite tea shop. It's in a side alley but very clean and very pleasant.'

'Lead on,' the Marques bowed.

The Tea and Cake people were very glad to see Clo again, especially looking her old self once more, not sad as she was last time. The dear Doctor. They bowed their heads for a respectful moment.

Clo, at a nod from Vincente, ordered jasmine tea and sugar cakes. It came on lovely old blue and white willow china. The Tea and Cake people stood round and smiled as Clo poured.

But at once, courteously, they withdrew, and Clo and Vincente could have been on a high, lonely mountain top by themselves.

'Well, Clotilda?' Vincente asked.

Clo thought back to what they had been talking about before they had come here and remembered Blasco and Aviella.

'No, not that subject,' Vincente dismissed, 'not boy meets girl, though Blasco is a little older than a boy now, and Aviella, as Isabella cattily likes to remark, was some grades senior than she was at school.'

'Then, *senhor*?'

'What is on your mind, what do you want to ask me?'

Clo stared at him. How could he have known that she needed his advice about Tang?

'Oh, I knew you had a worry, *pequena*,' he went on. 'Why did you not come to me before?'

'You were busy,' she said.

His hand shot across the table to imprison her hand. He held her hand so tightly that above and below the grasp the skin turned a drained white. He must have noticed it, for he released her hand at once.

'I am never too busy for you, Clotilda.' A pause. 'Well?'

'It's Tang,' she said again.

'Yes, Tang?'

Out it all burst, all about Dona Juanita taking the boy to Doctor Montales ... a blood disorder, such a loose diagnosis ... such an old doctor, even Maria had said so.

Then Clo babbled on that Harry had suggested the new American clinic, but she wasn't sure ... she felt she should ask ... Amah seemed quite calm over it all, just a little tiredness, Amah said. Clo made the gesture that Amah had, her two hands locked together and her head resting on them.

Then she stopped. She knew she must have made no sense.

But she had, it seemed.

'First of all, *senhorita*, let us be quite fair to Tia Juanita. Although she would say to you that she had taken the boy to the doctor it would not be so.'

'But she did, she did.'

'Socially only. The doctor is now a very old man, he has not accepted a case for some twenty years.'

'He looked at Tang,' Clo pointed out.

'Looked, but not examined. I imagine it went like this: Tia took tea with Montales, as she regularly does, small Tang probably took an iced bun. Then Tia drew Montales' attention to a listlessness she had noticed in the child, and the old doctor, bless him, said yes, possibly some blood disorder, I'll give him a mixture. But at no time would it be official, and at no time would Doctor Montales expect Tia to take his word—why, he would know she had her own doctor. So' ... a shrug ... 'at least let us deal fairly with Dona Juanita.'

'But has *she* been fair?' demanded Clo. 'Has she done what the doctor expected her to? Has she taken him elsewhere?'

'That,' promised Vincente, 'I intend to find out. And now on to other subjects. When this "boy" Blasco·met this "girl" Aviella, were you downcast?'

'Oh, heavens, no!' Clo had to laugh. 'I knew all along I was only a diversion for Blasco, that anything female not in a denim skirt and blouse——'

'Include in that a uniform and headband,' Vincente put in menacingly.

'—would set his eyes turning from me,' she finished.

'What did you do with those badges of office, Clo?'

'Badges of ... Oh, I obeyed you. I gave them away—such an expense! Three of them had never been worn.'

'They will be,' he assured her. 'Clopping along in her wooden pattens one day you will see someone in that dress instead of trousers and tunic, or a cheongsam, a matching band in her black hair.'

'Black silk hair,' admired Clo.

'I know of silk in another colour. The first young acorn, Clotilda.'

'The acorn that grows to a tree,' she smiled back.

For a long moment across the small table his black eyes held hers, held them until to Clo the two glances became only one glance ... the two people became one ... un- til——

'More tea?' asked Clo.

She did not see Vincente for several days. She saw Blasco, a very happy Blasco, wanting to talk to anyone who would listen to him on the subject of Aviella Martinez. It was not easy. Tia Juanita naturally had no wish to converse with the person she had brought out with Isabella in view, and Blasco plainly bored Isabella, in fact everything bored the Condessa except Harry, her future life with Harry.

'Isabella, are you sure?' Clo asked several times.

'Absolutely sure. I love him, Clo.'

'Less money for a while? Confined quarters, for educa- tional accommodation is not a palacio, Isabella?'

'Sackcloth, bread and water,' exulted Isabella. 'I love him, and that's my answer.'

'And what will Tia Juanita say?' Clo hated herself for saying that, but she felt it had to be said. For the first time Isabella's lovely face clouded.

'I love him,' she persisted, but her voice was not as exultant as before.

Clo saw Harry, and he was the same as Isabella, glad, yet somewhere there was something that Clo could not put a finger on. A kind of pre-dismay, she interpreted it. Oh, no, never dismay for that charming pair.

Vincente she did not see until the fourth evening, and

had she known, as Amah who had dressed Tang this morning had known, as Tia who had waved Tang off this morning had known, that Vincente had taken Tang to the Clinic, Clo would not have accepted his invitation to come into his study so casually.

Even after he had taken down two glasses and a bottle she was still casual, the Marques always indulged in a pre-dinner drink.

But this time it was no aperitif, no cocktail, no bright chatter light wine; it was brandy. And he poured his own and Clo's neat.

'Clotilda, I wish to say something to you. Sit very quiet, child.'

Now it was slowly reaching Clo, the seriousness was touching her. She held the stem of the glass tightly.

'Drink, *pequena*,' he persuaded.

'No.'

'It will be better if you do.'

'No, tell me, please. It's—Tang, isn't it?'

'Yes, little one, it is the child.'

Vincente began to speak.

The day outside faded. The study filled up with shadows. Presently it became quite dark in the room, and Vincente paused a moment to put on his desk lamp. It was a red lamp and its light shone rosily.

But as Vincente talked on there was no rose in Clo's heart, there was only grey.

CHAPTER TEN

CLO dawdled over changing her clothes, not out of impertinence but with the nervous hope that by the time she emerged the subject would be forgotten, the actors off the scene.

But she came back to the same setting, the only difference the absence of Blasco Ibanez. Senhor Ibanez had discreetly, and no doubt thankfully, left. But Vincente and Dona Juanita still waited.

Clo entered the room in the denim skirt and white blouse she favoured. She stood at the top of the several stairs above the sunken reception hall until the Marques autocratically nodded for her to descend.

'That's better,' he said in a more reasonable voice. 'What on earth got into you, child, to dress up like that?'

'The garments are very good,' she said defensively. 'They're silk.'

'So?' he said. He waited a moment. 'You have not answered me. Why did you come out pretending to be a personal maid?'

'The maids here wear black, *senhor*.'

'You are determined to be obstinate, I see. But please tell me one thing before we close this subject. Was this mode of dress—ordered?'

'Ordered?' she queried.

'Or obliged, or even suggested?'

'No, certainly not,' said Clo. 'Do I look the type to be ordered, obliged, suggested?' She could not have said why she reacted so vehemently; it was not Dona Juanita, she now actively disliked that lady. No, it was Vincente's overbearing approach.

'No hospitalisation? I mean not until——'

'Exactly. It might even come without hospitalisation, the Clinic said.'

'What else did they say?'

'Normal living. Nothing special. Days going on as they always go.'

'They were quite certain that—that——'

' "At this time and age and to the world's present medical knowledge," ' the Marques quoted quietly, ' "there is no known cure for this particular strain of leukaemia." That is what they said.'

'I see,' she said flatly.

'I have it planned like this,' Vincente told Clo. 'If that little life is to go on as it always has, then no one must know.'

'You and I know,' she pointed out.

'But I think we will use our knowledge wisely. What use would it be to tell Ah Seng?'

'No use,' agreed Clo, 'indeed, a sadness. She would weep a lot, and Tang would be upset. But Isabella? Harry?' A pause. 'Tia Juanita?'

'Isabella has only ever had casual touch with Tang, Harry as well. But Tia——'

'Yes? Tia?'

'Tia of all people must *not* know. She is an old lady now, Clo.'

'But when—if——'

'When—if—it happens? It is going to happen, Clotilda, and you must accept that.'

'Then when it happens?' she insisted.

'It will have happened, and the old lady will be more ready to accept it, for the simple reason that it *has* happened, that it is now over. Tell her before it is over and her heart will break ... Tang, sensing something, will be confused and disturbed.'

'I agree with you in all that, Vincente,' said Clo, 'but see my side. I, too, love the little boy, so why should I be deprived?'

'Deprived?' he questioned.

'Of his company, for if Dona Juanita doesn't know about his real condition she'll keep him away from me, as she's been keeping him away now for weeks.'

'Has she, Clo?'

'Yes.'

'Then I am sorry I was so blind I did not see. But do not worry now. She will keep him away no longer. I will get her to understand that that is not the right way, I will achieve this in a very discreet manner, suggest to Tia that Tang needs a younger approach when he is not with her or with his mother, I will say that it would be a good thing if you took over at times. Oh, she'll listen, Clotilda, have no fear about that. She always listens to me.'

'The great male?' she said drily.

'Perhaps.' He smiled for the first time and Clo smiled wanly back.

'But you, *pequena*,' he said presently, 'do you think you'll be able to carry it out?'

'Yes, I think I will. I'll be happy with him, I'll be interested, we'll go to places together. I shall point out to Tang that the Year of the Dragon is the merry year. It is, you know, the Dragon isn't a bad dragon at all, he's a kindly fellow. That fire that comes out of his nostrils isn't hot as you might think, and his claws are benign, the dragon only *looks* fierce. My old Amah told me that.'

'Then go, *pequena*, and tell the child.'

'Tell him about the kind dragon.' Clo's lip trembled, and it looked as though she would cry again. 'But he hasn't been a kind dragon to me, has he? Father, and now——'

'Perhaps these *are* his kindnesses,' Vincente said significantly. 'Who are we to know?'

Clo bit hard on the trembling lip and nodded. She was finding it difficult to think reasonably, and she knew the difficulty would continue. But she would try.

Evidently the Marques spoke to his aunt, for during the week Dona Juanita suggested to Clo that she take the little boy out at times.

'Vincente took Tang to the Clinic. Did you know?' the old lady asked.

'Yes.'

'A blood disorder, as Doctor Montales said.' Dona Juanita could not resist that thrust at Clo, yet she did it rather mildly. 'They suggested fresh air,' she continued, 'which, alas, because of my age, I cannot afford him, except in the car, and exercise, they assert, is the best way of attaining what they recommend. His mother seems always to be busy——'

'They are, Dona Juanita. They don't like modern methods, they prefer to work in the old laborious way.'

'So perhaps you could find time.'

'Yes,' promised Clo, 'I'll find time.'

Clo flew kites with Tang, noticing, sick at heart, how very little actual running he was doing now. She chased butterflies ... no, he corrected her gravely, he always chased dragonflies ... and again Clo noted how the chase was left to her.

Although he had preferred the pastime of running with a net, feeling, Clo always had thought, he was a cloud racing across the sky, now Tang began to favour fishing. Fishing was a slow, idle pastime, you sat on a bank and watched, and that was what Tang was doing now, watching the last few days of his few years go by.

Clo told him about the Year of the Dragon, and what a wonderful year it was, so much better than the dog year, or the rat year, the rest.

He asked in his pantomime mixture of Cantonese, Portuguese, English and hand gestures when he would see the Year of the Dragon again, and Clo said frozenly:

'You will be eighteen, Tang.'

She drew a dragon on his kite, embroidered a dragon on his overshirt, made him dragons out of coloured folding paper. They called the dragon Yut. Clo had suggested George as most suitable, but Tang wanted Yut.

'Yut is a very nice dragon name, Tang,' smiled Clo.

'Velly nice,' Tang agreed. He added proudly: *'Bom dias.'* He always said *Bom Dias* at the end of everything. Clo related this to Tia Juanita, with whom she was getting on much better lately, and the old lady laughed delightedly and spent her next session in the garden teaching Tang *boa tarde.*

'He is a quick boy,' she commented to Clo, 'he comprehended the difference at once. Tomorrow we will learn *adeus.'*

'Adeus, Dona Juanita?' said Clo with a stab at her heart. *Adeus,* she was thinking, is permanent, it is not just good-bye-see-you-again.

'Of course. He will soon learn that, too, he always does.'

Aviella had called up to the Villa Serra da Estrella, called several times, and it had become apparent, painfully, no doubt, that Dona Juanita had not brought out Blasco Ibanez for her blood niece but for her niece through marriage.

The pair, Aviella and Blasco, wasted no time. They announced their engagement at Aviella's third dinner at her aunt's, and Tia Juanita was polite but scarcely overjoyed.

Someone else was not overjoyed: Harry. Across the table, for the Professor was eating with the family tonight, Harry looked at Isabella, reminding her of something *she* had promised him, the announcement she and he had agreed upon, but an announcement as yet not voiced.

For a quivering moment Isabella looked back at Harry, then Isabella looked miserably away.

No announcement was made.

Barely conscious of all that was going on about her now, in her busy hours with Tang, Clo was made sharply aware of the position several days later. Isabella came to her white-lipped and near-distraught. Harry had left.

'Gone?' echoed Clo.

'His room in the annexe is empty,' Isabella told her.

'Just now it is,' Clo agreed, 'but he'll be lecturing.'

'He is not lecturing, I rang the college.'

'Then he has taken a class to the Gardens, or to the hills ...' The lecturers frequently did that, they believed that at times young brains wilted in the confines of four walls.

'No, he is gone. You see, he left a note.' Isabella handed it pitifully to Clo.

It was brutally direct, more like the Marques than the amiable Harry, Clo thought.

'As you cannot come to a point, I will. Goodbye. Harry.'

'Why didn't you, Isabella?' Clo asked. 'Why didn't you stand beside him if you love him?'

'There is no if—I do. But I found I couldn't, not to Tia.'

'You're still afraid of her?' asked Clo.

'No ... no. But—I love her. And she is old.'

Clo thought that over a while.

'So you lose Harry, Isabella?'

'Oh, no, Clo, no!'

'I'm sorry,' was all Clo could think to say, then she walked off. She *was* sorry, she was sorry to the ends of the earth for Isabella, but she knew she could not help; only Isabella could find her own way out of her self-made maze.

But if Clo had decided to let things take their course, to stand outside of it all, the young Condessa had other ideas.

She cornered Clo at every opportunity, imploring her to help, till Clo, grateful at least that Isabella was taking something else off her mind, diverting temporarily that ache that was Tang, at last agreed to see Harry.

But where to find him? She looked inquiringly at an unhelpful Isabella. When he had left here, if he had not gone to the hall of residence, then where?

'They would tell you,' cried Isabella. 'The college would tell you where they would never tell me. He will be rooming with another lecturer somewhere, or in a small flat.'

'Or a hotel handy to the airfield,' said Clo, 'handy for when he leaves for Honolulu.'

'No, Clo, no!' wailed Isabella.

'Isabella, you do realise I'm only going to find out something for you, not achieve a miracle.'

'I will do the miracle,' Isabella said in a quiet voice.

'What do you mean, Isabella?'

'Oh, Clo, find him! Find out. Tell me.'

Clo went down the next day to the hall of residence. The new family, one father, one mother and one little daughter, had moved into the Dennings' flat. They could have been the Dennings, Clo thought, twenty years ago. She talked with them for a while, then brought the subject round to Harry. Was his burned-out unit renewed yet?

'Renewed and occupied,' Clo was told. 'Professor Ferrier wouldn't have wanted the flat, anyway, he has applied successfully for a Hawaiian post.'

'Oh!' said Clo flatly. 'Would you know where Harry is now? Some other flat, I expect.'

'No, at a small hotel near the airport.'

So I was right, Clo sighed.

She went to the Kai Tak air terminal that afternoon, and had little trouble in finding Harry. He had chosen the least opulent of the inns, which was only to be expected, Clo thought, since lecturers' wages were not riches.

She was told which room, and she went up and knocked on the door. Harry opened up, and nodded her into a unit distinctively untidy as rooms are when about to be vacated. There was an open bag on his bed, and he was shoving things in.

Clo pushed him aside, and folded instead of crammed.

'You're really the very end!' she complained.

'Of course, Clotilda, but this *is* the end, the end of a dream, the end of everything for me.'

'Harry——' she began.

'It's no good trying to make me change my mind,' he said, 'so don't even start.'

'I'm not going to try, but I am critical of you making the break in such a discourteous way,' said Clo.

'Discourteous?' he queried.

'That's what I said. What has anybody up at the Peak done to you ... I mean, apart from Tia ... for you to slink away like this?'

'I'm not slinking, I'm simply going, no secret about it at all, and you needn't say apart from Tia, for she has done nothing at all, except, of course, be herself. But Isabella——'

'Wait, Harry,' counselled Clo earnestly.

'Yes?'

'Try to see it from Isabella's side.'

'Could you if you were me?' he said wryly.

Clo could not answer that, so she remained silent, and Harry could have rested on his laurels, but he chose to go further.

'Would it have happened if you were Isabella?' he demanded.

'I don't know. But I do know that if the parent figure had been Dad, I, too, might be doing what Isabella is doing now.'

'Which is?'

'Breaking her heart.'

'Oh, come off it, Clo, Tia is never the old Doctor.'

'I said parent figure,' she corrected, 'but I agree, she's not. But it still doesn't end at that, and you of all people should be able to understand.'

'Understand what?' he asked.

'The family tie you've always yearned for. You never had it, and now you're asking Isabella to relinquish hers.'

'I'm not. Good grief, I'm not that horrendous! I'm simply asking her to summon up enough guts to go and say: "I love you, Aunt, but my husband comes first." We're not breaking anything off, Clo, far from it—why, I'd quite like to be someone's nephew. But I can't be unless a first step is taken, and one minute Isabella is ready to take the step, and the next minute she's in floods of tears. I tell you, Clo, I've had it. This is the very end.'

'Harry——' she began.

'No. *No*. You can tell the Condessa Isabella, little messenger girl, that she can't have her cake and eat it.'

'I'm no messenger girl, Harry, though Isabella did ask me to try to help.'

'There's only one thing that will help, Clo,' he added.

'Yes, I know,' nodded Clo, 'and I'll pass it on. I see your side, Harry, and you're right, of course, but, as the daughter of my father ... and a dear mother, though I can't remember her ... I can see Isabella's side, too. You think Isabella is afraid of Tia, don't you?'

'I do, and no wonder, she is rather a gorgon. But Isabella is a woman now, and should be able to overcome that.'

'Yes ... but you never overcome love, Harry.'

'Isabella has no love in her,' he said flatly.

'You never get over family, and associations, and——'

'You're speaking to an orphan, remember, kid. All right, Clo, clear out.' He went as though to give Clo a push to help her out, but instead he gave her a peck. 'Oh, girl, girl,' he sighed, not far from tears.

Clo went back to the Villa Serra da Estrella and reported

everything. She added nothing, but she left out nothing.

After that she went out herself, feeling absolutely depleted, and started thinking about Tang again, the first time really in days. There was something to be said about new worries, she smiled wanly, for a while at least they brought a cessation of an old pain. How much longer of *this* pain, how long?

When she saw Tang, she was happily surprised. He seemed better than when she had last seen him, more deeply golden, the glow in his perfect little cheeks warmer and rosier. But then the wave always surges stronger before it ebbs for ever. Where had she heard that? Clo frowned.

But there was no frowning with Tang. Tia had bought him a wind-up musical box, and he showed Clo with pride. He even made would-be musical sounds to it, up and down, tintinnabular notes that mean melody to the Cantonese, he sang words that he did not understand but had learned parrot-wise.

'Here we go gathering nuts in May
On a cold and flosty morning.'

'You and your flost!' smiled Clo, hugging him to her.

Above his little bullet-head Clo saw two pairs of eyes watching her. The Marques was bringing his aunt down the path to the summer house, and the couple had paused.

The old lady's look was cold and displeased, it resented Clo. But Vincente's look was warm and embracing, it embraced Clo as though his two arms had reached out and folded her in.

Flushing, she gave Tang a gentle little push towards the old lady, and went back to the house.

That night all hell ... Clo could only call it that ... was let loose.

At dinner Isabella did not make an appearance, but, apart from tightening her already tight lips, Tia Juanita made no sign of disapproval.

'We will proceed,' was all she said.

Harry, of course, was not there, had not been for a week now, but Aviella and Blasco were present—Blasco to speak later to Vincente on his new assignment, for Blasco now was 'in' the firm—Aviella just to radiate triumphant happiness, or so it seemed.

There was no secret about Isabella's dislike of Aviella, so Isabella's absence now was taken by Dona Juanita simply as a discourtesy. A grave discourtesy, but nothing else. The old lady suspected nothing.

Nothing was suspected, either, when Isabella did not join the ladies in the drawing room, or the men and the ladies afterwards in the larger reception room.

Tia, indeed, would have gone to bed without any questioning, just with an icy disapproving face, had not the girl who attended Isabella come to her with the inquiry as to whether she should wait up for the Condessa. Should she draw her bath, turn down her bed?

'She is not in her room?'

'No, Dona Juanita.'

'You fool of a girl, why did you not tell me earlier?' demanded the old lady.

'I thought you would know. Also, I thought she might come.'

'I didn't know, and she hasn't come—No, Vincente, I will not be silent.' Vincente, sensitive for the girl, was trying to silence his aunt.

'She must be somewhere. If she has gone out, why hasn't she telephoned? Tell me' ... turning so angrily on the girl that the unfortunate maid withdrew a step ... 'is there a message left?'

'No, no message, senhora. But——'

'Then she is just being difficult, and I will have something to say to her—No, Vincente, I will not be quiet—She may be a woman now, and a Condessa, but——' A quick look at the girl. 'You said no message, yet you seemed to indicate something. Is there anything else to be said?'

'Yes, Dona Juanita. Some clothes are gone. And—and a bag.'

It all began then. Dona Juanita walked up and down, the pale, aristocratic countenance above the collaret of pearls twisted, distorted. She forgot she needed a silver-topped stick and she brushed any help from Vincente angrily aside.

She told Aviella and Blasco to go home, and Clo waited to be sent packing, too, but the old lady did not do that; she wanted words with her first.

Miss Denning had connived all this, of course. She had set her cap at the Marques ... again Vincente was withered into silence ... but when that failed, as, of course, it would fail, Vincente being who he was, in sheer spite she had turned her attention on Isabella and her fellow ... a downward turn of the mouth ... Australian.

'How dared you do this?' she stormed. 'What do you raw Australians think you are? Our Portuguese navigators founded Brazil, they colonised India, we are an old and proud people. Your father spoke often of his admiration of our country, but his daughter——'

'His daughter doesn't,' came in Clo thickly. She felt quite sickened. 'I can only speak disparagingly of them, of Isabella who caused all this commotion by being such a clinging vine, of Blasco, who has to ask a fellow country-man for a post, of Aviella who's been looking for a husband, of you, who must be the nastiest old woman in the world, of the Marques whom I wouldn't have if he was the last man in creation!'

'*He*, Senhorita Denning, would not have *you*!'

'Oh, yes, I would, Tia. I would indeed.' The Marques had stepped forward, and in doing so he intentionally but kindly pushed the old lady aside. 'I would have her and I would cherish her, but my God, just now I feel more like slapping her. You are a young woman, Clotilda,' he turned to her, 'and you take notice of an old lady.' You should be ashamed!'

Tia was standing incredulous, the maid who still had not left stood frankly delighted. Blasco and Aviella, still not gone, looked at each other, then the pair of them crept out.

Tia broke the silence.

'Something must be done,' she said, but her voice now was controlled, and all the fire had gone out of her.

'It has been done, I'm afraid,' Clo proffered, and her voice, too, was quiet. 'I think I can hear the plane.'

'To where, Clotilda?' It was Vincente.

'Honolulu. Harry has got a job there.'

'And taken Isabella?' It was Dona Juanita now.

'The last time I saw him that was *not* in his plans, or hers,' said Clo.

'... No, but it crept in later.' A voice spoke at the door and they all turned. Harry and Isabella stood there. Dona Juanita gave a little cry and made a half step forward, then she stopped.

'It wasn't in my plans,' Harry repeated. 'I admit it was at first, but Isabella refused, so I decided to go alone. I loved her, she loved me, but she found she couldn't leave her family in such a way, in such a state of—well, *un*love.

'But tonight she came to the airport to tell me she'd changed her mind. She even brought her bags.

'I was overjoyed. I was rapturous. Then ... well, something Clo had said to me came back.'

'Yes, Harry?' asked Vincente. 'What did this child say?'

'She said you never overcome love. Isabella loved me, but Isabella loved her family, too. To someone who had never had that, it was hard to understand ... I mean, it was hard to understand until I remembered how *I* had always wanted to belong, and how, if I did, I would never let my belonging go.'

'Yet Isabella did?' asked Vincente softly.

'Isabella did. But now I'm bringing her back. Not for ever, not even for more than a few days, but long enough, we hope, for the one who has called Isabella back to her to understand, and to kiss her and let her go. Either that' ... a sidewise look ... 'or accept me as well.' Now Harry turned fully to Tia Juanita.

But the old lady was not ready yet. She was mollified, she was even ashamed, but she was not ready. Would that proud old lady ever be ready?

'The annexe awaits you, Harry,' the Marques said quietly.

'I've re-booked at my hotel,' Harry told him.

'For how long?'

'The next flight out, perhaps the one after that, no longer.'

'Then goodnight, old fellow.'

'Goodnight, Vincente.' Harry turned now to the ladies 'Dona Juanita.' A bow. 'See you, Clo.' No bow. He did not speak to Isabella. He did not need to.

He went out, and Isabella went to her room, Dona Juanita to hers.

Clo waited until the Marques went to the garages to arrange transport for Harry, then she went to her own unit. But she did not undress. She found herself listening for a knock on the door, for Vincente to come.

There was no knock. Clo waited and waited. She saw the lights go out one by one until only the patio and the hall lights remained.

At last she, too, went to bed.

CHAPTER TWELVE

THE next day everything seemed to function automatically, everyone went around mechanically.

The meals appeared, were touched, were cleared away. The maids moved silently and efficiently as they always did, and if they were curious, as they must be curious after what Isabella's young girl undoubtedly had told them, they never showed it.

Contrary to Clo's anticipations Dona Juanita came down for both lunch and dinner ... she had always breakfasted in her room ... Clo rather had expected her to retire to her suite and have everything brought to her there.

But not this magnificent old lady. She walked as proud and erect as ever, was meticulously polite and correct ... and cold as ice.

She never lingered after meals, she returned to her room at once, and this gave Clo more time with Tang, something she had wanted badly, but now that she had it, found herself wishing that Tia could join her. She even toyed with the idea of going to Tia and pleading: 'Please come, before it's too late.'

But that would entail offering a reason, something that the Marques had said should not be given, and Clo had agreed. So thankfully, yet sadly, sad for an autocratic old woman, she spent hours with Tang, most of the hours, now that tiredness had caught up with him, with Tang leaning against her knee, singing a lethargic Nuts in May to his music box, finishing it with *Bom dias, Boa tarde* ... *Adeus*. Yes, he now knew *Adeus*. Not a happy 'till we meet again' ... not a cheery 'see you some time' ... but farewell. *Adeus*.

There was no butterfly ... no, Tang corrected still, *dragonfly* ... netting any more, and even to go to the stream was an ordeal. Mostly they stayed by the lily pond watching small birds settling on the lily pads, taking off again.

Tang slept a great deal, so Clo got into the habit of carrying a light rug and a pillow with her, and when inertia took him she would make up a little crib wherever he was. It was under a bauhinia tree in full mauve and blue blossom that Isabella found the pair of them one afternoon.

'In Europe they call this the Judas tree.' Isabella reached up and picked one of the purple-blue flowers.

'Put it behind the correct ear,' Clo advised.

'Which ear is it for someone who doesn't know when she's being married but knows she is?'

'Oh, Isabella!' Clo smiled with her.

'Yes, it's wonderful. At least it would be if Tia would come round. Do you think she ever will?'

'I don't know. Shall you wait?'

'A few days more, Clo. Harry has had his appointment put back for a week, but he says not a minute more. And I' ... confidently ... 'would not allow it to be any more.'

'But you would like a more pleasant farewell?'

'Oh, yes. I have no doubt that somewhere in the years to come Tia will relent, especially if I produce a child, but I'd like it now, I'd like it before, not after.'

'But you won't let it make a difference?'

'No, Clo, never again. I expect' ... diffidently ... 'you've been fairly sickened of me.'

'Never,' Clo assured her. 'I've put myself in your place, and Dad in Tia's.'

'Your father was another person altogether. Tia ... well, how can I describe Tia?'

'As not belonging to these times.'

'Yes. She was educated entirely at home, if you can call

embroidery and art and ladylike accomplishments education.'

'Yet she was extremely interested in the Doctor,' Clo reminded her.

'Probably because of all that embroidery and art when she would sooner have had literature or mathematics or whatever. She was reared in the old ways that have gone out now, fortunately gone out. I think she must be the last grand old lady.'

'And she tried to pass it all on to you.'

'Yes. Poor Tia—Sometimes I feel terribly ashamed of myself, Clo,' Isabella confessed. 'When I agreed to her advice and married the Conde, it was not really because of Tia, it was because a Condessa I would "up" Tia, who was only Dona Juanita. My own aunt would be a lesser rank.'

'You were a minx!' scolded Clo.

'Perhaps. Quite often I actively disliked Tia, I recall, but always it came down to that love–hate relationship again, as it is now, but with love generally on top.'

'And you expect her to love you back?'

'Just nod me off would do, the love can come from Harry—Clo, that child does not look well.'

'. . . No, Isabella, Tang is ill.'

'Very ill?'

'Yes,' said Clo flatly.

'I'm sorry.' Isabella bit her lip. 'Does Tia know?'

'Vincente said no.'

'Then the small one is . . . he must be . . .'

'Yes.'

'Oh.' Two tears ran down Isabella's lovely cheeks, and Clo longed for similar release. Since that first night when Vincente had told her, her eyes had burned with dryness.

To carry on with the promptness of their romance, Aviella

and Blasco were being married almost at once.

'I am leaving Blasco in command here in Hong Kong,' Vincente told Clo the next morning. 'Aviella is not exactly Tia's favourite niece, but at least she will be company to the old lady when Isabella finally gets away.'

'Yes, that's a good idea. Dona Juanita needs someone permanent on hand, for you are so often away.'

'Yes, Clotilda, we frequently will be away.'

'We?' Clo looked at him in inquiry, but received no reply.

That afternoon Clo, watching Tang, decided that she *must* include Dona Juanita whatever Vincente thought. She sought him out.

'Tang's cheeks are thinning ... he has this strained look. I know it will upset Tia, but I am sure she must notice it soon,' she said anxiously.

'Have no fears of that,' he reassured her. 'Tia's eyes are bad, she is so proud she will not wear the spectacles she should. All she will see of Tang will be what she always saw, and wants to see. Golden cheeks, soft dark eyes. Dimpled hands.'

'The dimples are going,' sighed Clo.

'Tia will still see them.'

'It's going to be a great shock to her. Vincente, are we doing right?'

'She is a deeply religious woman and will accept,' he said. 'Yes, I think this way is best.'

Now Clo asked Vincente a question she had wanted to ever since she had heard the news.

'Senhor—' she began.

'Yes, *pequena*?'

'We know how it will be with Amah, with Dona Juanita, with us, but how will it be—with Tang?'

'Ah, I have wanted you to ask that. He will be tired, the doctors have told me, very, *very* tired. They described it for

a small child as rolling, as children like to roll, down a
gentle slope, then stopping at the bottom resting, glad they
don't have to roll any more.'

'No pain?'

'Not as medical science has planned it for this little
flower.'

'Just resting?'

'Just resting, Clotilda.'

Tang died in the late afternoon. He rolled down the gentle
slope and reached the bottom, and then the flower was
gone.

Vincente must have persuaded Tia Juanita to abandon
her room and take some air, for after tea she went and sat,
like old times, in the summer house. Clo brought Tang to
her there, then went away. As she left she heard Tang
weakly winding up his musical box.

Clo came back several times, and on the first occasion
Tang looked a little better, and was repeating after Tia
'Bom dias' ... 'Boa tarde' ... 'Adeus.'—Adeus? The
second time he was playing with Tia's rosary, he liked to
do that, and singing, 'On a cold and flosty morning', and
the third...

The third time he had left them, left them so quietly that
Tia did not know. But Clo saw and knew, and she came
and took Tang in her arms.

At once Tia's brows rose haughtily, then she saw Clo's
crumpled face, and her old face crumpled, too. As Clo carried the light little boy, so light he could have been a
butterfly in his butterfly net, the old lady dropped to her
knees in the garden and began fingering her beads.

As light as a butterfly ... no, Clo heard Tang correcting,
a dragonfly ... as light as a little wind scattering clouds
across heaven.

... 'How far, I wonder, did he stray
    Chasing the burnished dragonfly today?'

How far is the chase, Tang? she asked achingly. Darling,
I hope you catch your dragonfly.

'So it's *adeus*.' Vincente had come in beside Clo, and he
gently and finally pulled up the sheet of the little boy's cot.

Somewhere outside Clo could hear Amah, who must
have been told, wailing loudly, blubbering, crying for
everyone to hear.

'She'll do it for two days,' Clo said tonelessly. 'Then life
will start again. It's a good way, really—father told me
that. There's no futility, he said, like the futility of grief.
But oh, oh, I'll miss him!'

'We will all miss him, Clotilda. We will all miss him
very much.'

'Perhaps I could go to Dona Juanita——'

'No,' Vincente said, 'Isabella and Harry are doing that.
A life has been taken, a life is given. Two lives for Tia—
Isabella, Harry. Tia is turning to them—But Clotilda,
what of our life? Have you thought of that?'

But Clo could think of nothing. A rending, aching misery
had taken possession of her, it was useless pointing out that
if it had to be, it was better this way; all she could feel was
pain, an enormity of pain.

In the end Vincente took her to her room and put her on
her bed. He held a glass to her lips and made her drink.
There must have been a strong sedative in it, for Clo began
to drift almost at once. As she floated away she saw Vincente's concerned face, but the voice she heard was Tang's.

Bom dias. Boa tarde. Adeus.

'A little gold boy,' Clo mumbled, 'chasing dragonflies in
heaven.'

She slept.

*

In exactly two days Amah had stopped her lamenting, her loud, unabashed weeping and sobbing, and put on a fresh tunic, washed her face, neatened her already neat hair, put in its gilt pin, then presented herself to Tia Juanita.

'All over,' she said.

Clo was with Tia at the time, indeed she was with her often now, and she was as surprised as the old lady when Ah Seng added to her announcement that she would like to leave.

This was a good job, Clo knew, and Cantonese do not easily relinquish a position, but Amah was obviously going without regrets. She had only stayed on, she said, because of Tang, Tang had been so fond of Lady—Amah bowed.

But now there was no need to stay any more ... a cousin of her dead husband's cousin had offered Ah Seng a house in the country. She would have all her children round her.

Clo knew it was a blow to Dona Juanita. Although she had not mentioned it, Tia had taken it for granted that First or Third Son would arrive one day to take Second Son's place, and, although he would never be their own sweet dreamer, he would be young and soft-eyed and ... most important to the old lady ... male. But now there was not to be any little follow-up.

'Of course you must do as you wish, Ah Seng,' Dona Juanita said.

'And take Tang's pretty clothes you gave to him? And take singing box, please?' Ah Seng spoke good English.

'Yes. Yes. Make a parcel of them, Clotilda.' No longer was Clo Senhorita Denning, she was Clotilda.

Clo obeyed.

Vincente was away on business, but Blasco and Aviella called in frequently, and were greeted a shade more warmly by Tia. But only a shade. Clo, too, although she was accepted, could not call it more than that, than toleration.

Then came the first breakthrough. Harry came up from

the college one day and instantly cornered Isabella. There could be no more delays, he said, a cable had come saying he must take up residence at once in Hawaii or he would forfeit the post.

'Then,' said Isabella calmly, 'we will be married at once. But first let me speak with Tia.'

'You won't——' he began.

'Oh, no, I won't, Harry. Not ever again.'

Isabella was a long time in her aunt's room, but when at last she came out, she was smiling. And coming behind her, leaning on her silver-topped stick, was Tia Juanita. She stood there haughty and unapproachable for a full minute, then she spoke.

'What is everyone standing around for? Are marriages something that happen every day, then? We shall, of course, have the reception here. Ring Aviella, Clotilda, you will need her, and while you do that tell her to advise Blasco to contact Vincente. He will know where he is.

'Compile a list of caterers. Order flowers. We will need a red carpet. Professor, where are you? Come here!'

Harry went.

'I would like it,' said the old lady, 'at the Cathedral.'

'Any church you say,' he assured her, 'even the little one round the corner.'

'There is none around the corner, and besides, it must be, of course, in the Cathedral.'

'I don't care,' mumbled Harry, 'if we just climb up to the top of the Peak and call out to the world that we're now man and wife.'

'Harry!' reproved Clo, but ... and Clo could not credit it ... Tia gave a shadow of a smile.

'You young girls will require new gowns,' she said. 'Please to ring Chung Wong.'

'I've always had Lee Lan,' Clo proffered.

'Chung Wong. I will wear my black silk, naturally, but

the collaret of diamonds. All right, what are you all doing standing around?'

They sprang to action. Between them they arranged for the Cathedral, for the priest, for flowers to supplement the villa's own abundance of flowers, for caterers, though for the more personal Portuguese touches Dona Juanita had long audiences with her cook ... the dresses.

Isabella, as a second time bride, must not wear white, a fact which pleased Chung Wong, for white to the Cantonese meant mourning, and this was a marriage. He very much approved of the Condessa's choice of glowing rose.

When it came to Clo's turn, she was indecisive. Blue? Buttercup? Lilac?

'Green,' decided Dona Juanita, 'the same green as the first time I saw you, Clotilda. It suited you.'

... I was a young oak tree, Clo remembered that from Vincente. I stopped being an acorn and I grew up for a night.

So green it was.

Isabella's wedding day dawned brightly, but then weather was fairly predictable in Hong Kong. In spring it was wise to keep a jacket handy, in summer most of the rainfall was recorded, in autumn the days were clear and in winter sometimes you needed a coat.

Now was the perfect time of the year, early autumn, and the best season.

Clo rejoiced about this to Isabella, but Isabella frowned slightly.

'Yet,' she said a little worried, 'Signal Hill is indicating the probability of strong winds.' Signal Hill was Hong Kong's warning station, from it came the dreaded symbols of approaching typhoons.

'Signal Hill?' disbelieved Clo. 'But it's not typhoon time.' But even as she said it she remembered reading in an

Australian paper that cyclones had occurred out of season Down Under this year.

'I'm torn,' admitted Isabella. 'Harry and I want to get out before anything breaks, but on the other hand we'll be consumed with worry for everyone back here.'

'Not on the Peak,' denied Clo. 'We look down on disaster up here, not meet it.' She had crossed to the window that looked far below to the harbour, and all at once she shivered. She knew, from past typhoons, what ruin, what heartbreak a typhoon can bring.

But this was crisp, sweet autumn, barely autumn, more Indian summer really. It couldn't happen now.

The wedding went off perfectly. There was only a small number of guests, for Isabella had few Hong Kong friends and Harry none at all. The great dark Cathedral, much too large for the small party, echoed the sound of their footsteps, echoed Harry's proud promises, Isabella's shy ones.

Blasco was standing beside Harry and opposite to Clo. During a prayer Clo heard a faint rustle of steps, and when she got to her feet again, Blasco had joined his Aviella in a pew, and Vincente stood there.

All through the service Vincente did not take his eyes off Clo, warm, dark eyes, and suddenly it came exultantly to her that besides Isabella and Harry being married, she was being married to Vincente.

Yet it couldn't be, of course. Harry had married Isabella, but Harry was a man of letters, an esteemed lecturer; in years to come he would be Doctor Denning all over again. But she was Clotilda, nothing much, her only mark of esteem her once-esteemed father; she was ... she was an acorn. He, that man pretending marriage with her, saying it with his warm rich gaze, had told her that. 'You are an acorn.'

'Are you ready, little green oak?' Vincente said softly. 'The procession is moving off.'

Back at the Villa Sera da Estrella everything went off as Dona Juanita had ordered it. The bride, even though she was a bride in pink, was crowned, and Harry, looking sheepish, was crowned as well.

The two rings that had been exchanged in the church were removed, placed on a velvet cushion, and a Portuguese priest from Macao this time added his prayers.

The cake was cut, the wine drunk. A little heady from it all, Clo did not notice the sky getting darker.

However, nothing happened before the young couple got away, indeed, Aviella, Blasco, Clo and Vincente were back from seeing them off at the air terminal before the first stir of wind, the first uneasy writhing of trees and shrubs.

Then within minutes, no more, the typhoon struck.

CHAPTER THIRTEEN

THE uneasy writhing of the trees changed to an agonised distorting and twisting. The winds began rattling every window, the rain, that had now begun, thrust downward in sharp needles. The bauhinia and temple trees leaned over in tortured semi-circles. Leaves, sticks and stones were crashed against the villa in a dreadful cannonade.

One large casuarina was uprooted, lifted, then dropped again on the summer house. The rain began to drive horizontally, and several windows crashed. The noise was thunderous. It was like discharging metal. When the wind dislodged a tree it seemed as if a gargantuan wave was breaking against a cliff.

The silver javelins of rain thickened monstrously, then shrieked, roared, plunged and cut viciously at anything left standing, for within ten minutes, even less, there was little standing, except the villa and those in it. The summer house, the trees, the shrubs, the flowers, the lily pond were all gone.

Frightening though it was, what they saw through the few remaining windows was far more awful. Down in the harbour, between the flashes of light and the swirls of rain, they could see sampans and junks racing across to the Kowloon typhoon shelter, but it did not need their close attention to know that many would not get there.

Then Vincente shut his eyes a moment and Dona Juanita said 'Dear God', and Clo knew that even the junks and sampans that had made the shelter were doomed.

A great wave was running in, spray running with it, and it was crumbling up the waterfront as though each building was only a matchbox. Brown water swirled everywhere.

Landslides sprung from all directions. There was collapse and rubble and utter ruin.

'...And now it is over,' Vincente said not long after. Typhoons were usually like that, they came, they destroyed, they went on for more destruction.

'Is it?' cried Clo, looking down pitifully.

'The typhoon has roared over to Central China. Now' ... grimly ... 'the work begins. I will go, of course, Tia.'

'Yes, yes, go, Vincente.'

'Clotilda.' He did not come across to Clo, he simply bent his head.

'Be careful,' she said.

'What else?' he asked, and he went out of the Villa Serra da Estrella.

They did not hear from Vincente the rest of the day, nor the morning after.

The telephone wires were down, so there was no communication, unless one descended by the cable tram which was now running again.

Clo's message from the college came through the cable car. Heng, who had been their general rouseabout in the hall of residence, came up in it with a letter from the Director.

'Clo, we have been asked by the University to join with them in general restoration. Remembering how you always were a tower of strength in the old days, especially with the kids, I'm asking you to help swell our ranks now. Heng will conduct you down, but only by cable car, all our own cars are out. S.O.S. Fothergill.'

'Wait here, Heng.' Clo crossed to Dona Juanita's room and tapped on the door.

She knew what she was going to say, and she didn't care if the old lady liked it or not, and she would not like it. She would expect permission to be asked, not a declaration made.

'Dona Juanita, I'm going down to help,' she announced.

'But I anticipated that, Clotilda.' And as Clo had done with Vincente, the old lady said:

'Be careful.'

On an impulse, Clo went across and took the old hand and kissed it.

'I will,' she promised.

Outside it looked as though a monstrous comb had been tugged through the entire city. There was ruin and wreckage everywhere. Trees were uprooted in their thousands. Small roads had slipped away, larger roads had collapsed. Roofs were off, windows in sharp splinters. People already were wandering stoically among the ruins to try to identify their things.

The cable car descended at a snail's pace, every few minutes it was checked, or some new wreckage taken off its rails.

At the bottom everything looked flattened, but even this soon after the storm, stalls, temporarily supported, were being strung up, then manned by people determined to help.

Heng and Clo went straight to the hall of residence, and here Mr Fothergill said he would like Clo to go to the small east orphanage where she had worked last time. She would be a help there, she knew what was needed, but no one could be called upon to take her.

'No,' said Clo, 'I can walk.'

But it proved quite a long walk. Time after time she had to detour because rubble stopped her. It was almost an hour before she finally came to the home.

She stood a moment in horror, gazing at the utter desolation of the small place. Practically only the name remained, a row of Chinese lettering, that Doctor Denning once had told Clo 'boiled down' meant waifs and strays.

'Not literally, of course, Clo,' he had added, 'the Cantonese are too kind for that, but only the absolute un-belonging ones would be brought here.'

There were very few around now, and Clo was wondering where else she could make herself useful when the welfare worker saw her. She was English, and had known Clo for years.

'We moved them on,' she reassured. 'Quite a good place, I think, better than this ever was. But then what happens?' The welfare worker spread her hands.

'Yes, Sister Dorothy?'

'One atom left out—a small girl. I just don't know what to do with her. I've so much work I can't turn, and this crops up.'

'This' she then brought forward. The tiniest child Clo could imagine, at least the tiniest walking one, dark cream skin, dark eyes, hair cut square with a window pane front, small hands, smaller feet.

'I don't even know who she is,' the welfare worker said, 'and she can't tell.'

'Belonging?' asked Clo.

'Definitely un-belonging. All these children are.'

'Can I take her?'

'I was waiting for that,' Sister Dorothy said. She bent down and picked up the child and handed her to Clo. She wasn't even that light weight that Tang had been before he died.

Clo carried her back to the cable car. The little girl neither resisted nor responded, she just remained in Clo's arms.

Travelling up in the tram, Clo tried to talk to her, she knew a little Cantonese. But it evidently was not the baby's Cantonese.

When they reached the villa, Clo found Dona Juanita in the sitting room, looking down on the toffee-dark harbour waters with distress.

'I did not expect you so soon,' the old lady began ... then she stopped. 'What is this?'

'A child who was evidently not evacuated with the other children,' Clo told her.

'Evacuated from where?'

'A waifs' home.'

'She is an orphan?'

'Yes. Until they can find out what group she was assigned to, I thought we could keep her here.'

'And afterwards let her go?' Dona Juanita asked.

'Yes ... yes, I suppose so.'

'Isn't that a sad thing to suppose?'

'It is, but how could I help?' asked Clo.

'You could help now by asking—me.'

'I thought that. I wanted that.' Clo looked at the old lady eagerly but disbelievingly. 'You need a child now that Tang has gone, but—but, Dona Juanita, this is a little girl.'

'With hair like that, of course. The Hong Kong boys are bullet-cropped. And what is wrong with a girl?'

'Nothing ... nothing. But you prefer boys.'

'Only for lineal purposes,' said Dona Juanita crisply. Then she said: 'And I think Isabella and the Professor may be able to help me there, and if not, Vincente.'

'Most certainly Vincente.' The Marques had come in so softly that Clo had not heard him. His work must have been done. 'What do you say, Clotilda?'

'What do I say? There's nothing for me to say. But, Dona Juanita do you mean it? Will you really accept this little girl child?'

'She is accepted already, you foolish child yourself. What is her name?'

'I've asked her,' said Clo, 'and she doesn't seem to know.'

The sun had come out, and after all the rain it was very humid.

'Where is my fan?' the old lady complained.

'Fan. Fan.' The little girl came across to her. She looked up at her and said: 'Fan' again. She began playing with Dona Juanita's rosary beads, just as Tang had played.

'She is Ah Fan,' discovered Tia with delight, 'and she is also a lotus flower.'

But it was still not enough for Clo.

'If Isabella and Harry have a daughter, what then?' she asked with concern for the little fairy.

'That is true, Tia.' The Marques had joined Clo. 'What if *we* have a daughter?'

'Then there will be three girls,' snapped Dona Juanita. 'Can't you count?'

'All loved?' persisted Clo.

The old lady looked up from the little square head with the window pane hair cut and said:

'Yes. All loved.'

What happened then, Clo afterwards could not remember. She knew that Dona Juanita took Ah Fan on her lap and began talking to her, probably already teaching her *Bom dias* and *Boa tarde*. Clo could not be sure of that.

But she was sure of strong arms guiding her out of the room, on to the patio ... where she had been guided one night. It seemed a long time ago now.

It was dark by now, a quiet and beautiful dark after ugliness and destruction. Clo did not resist when the Marques drew her into an alcove, a little corner where a potted palm had once stood.

'We started something last time,' he said, 'but we never finished it. This time we do finish it, Clotilda.'

He pulled her close ... closer ... then he deliberately began running his fingertips through her hair at the temples, then moving his long sensuous fingers over her shoulders, quite slowly and rather lightly at first, then quicker and stronger. He traced the line of her slender backbone up and down, touched the hollow of her throat, and then at last his mouth came forward to kiss hers.

Commanding yet gentle, steel strong yet pulsing, in this Year of the Dragon he did.

Have you missed any of these best-selling Harlequin Romances?

By popular demand... to help complete your collection of Harlequin Romances

48 titles listed on the following pages...

Harlequin Reissues

Harlequin Reissues

Complete and mail this coupon today!